D0036746

Dear Reader,

What better way to keep warm on these brisk November nights than being caught up in the four adrenaline-pumping romances Silhouette Intimate Moments has for you!

USA TODAY bestselling author Merline Lovelace starts off the month with *Closer Encounters* (#1439), the latest installment in her CODE NAME: DANGER miniseries. An undercover agent and a former D.A. must work together, all while fighting a consuming attraction, to solve a sixty-year-old murder. RITA® Award-winning author Catherine Mann continues her WINGMEN WARRIORS series with *Fully Engaged* (#1440). To save a woman from his past, an Air Force warrior must face his worst nightmares.

Popular author Cindy Dees delights us with *The Lost Prince* (#1441), where a Red Cross aide must risk her life and her heart to help an overthrown prince save his crumbling nation. And be sure to read *A Sultan's Ransom* (#1442), the second book in Loreth Anne White's SHADOW SOLDIERS trilogy. Here, a mercenary and a doctor must team up to stop a deadly biological plague from wreaking havoc on the world.

Over the next few months, watch as Silhouette Intimate Moments brings exciting changes to its covers, and look for our new name, Silhouette Romantic Suspense, coming in February 2007. As always, we'll deliver on our promise of breathtaking romance set against a backdrop of suspense. Have a wonderful November, and happy reading!

Sincerely,

Patience Smith
Associate Senior Editor

Please address questions and book requests to:
Silhouette Reader Service
U.S.: 3010 Walden Ave., P.O. Box 1325, Buffalo, NY 14269
Canadian: P.O. Box 609, Fort Erie, Ont. L2A 5X3

CATHERINE MANN

Fully Engaged

Silhouette

INTIMATE MOMENTS™

Published by Silhouette Books

America's Publisher of Contemporary Romance

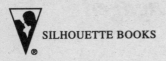

SILHOUETTE BOOKS

ISBN-13: 978-0-373-27510-6
ISBN-10: 0-373-27510-2

FULLY ENGAGED

Books by Catherine Mann

Silhouette Intimate Moments

*Wingmen Warriors

CATHERINE MANN

Five-time RITA® Award finalist Catherine Mann pens contemporary military romances, a natural fit since she's married to her very own Air Force flyboy. Since June 2002 she has won the Romance Writers of America's prestigious RITA® Award and the Booksellers Best Award, as well as being a finalist for *Romantic Times BOOKclub*'s Reviewer's Choice Award. A former theater-school director and university teacher, Catherine graduated from the College of Charleston with a B.A. in fine arts: theater and received her master's degree in theater from UNC Greensboro. Now, following her aviator husband around the world with four children, a beagle and two tabbies in tow offers endless inspiration for new stories. For more information, visit her Web site at www.catherinemann.com or write her at P.O. Box 6065, Navarre, FL 32566.

In memory of Jeri Houghton and Susan Jeglinski.
You are remembered.

And to Harlequin/Silhouette author Bonnie Gardner.
I appreciate more than I can express your sharing details
of your breast cancer recovery journey. Your strength and
courage humble me. (Any mistakes about breast cancer
treatment and recovery are my own. To learn more about
breast cancer detection and treatment, I hope you'll visit the
American Cancer Society's Web site at www.cancer.org.)

Acknowledgments:

I've long wanted to tell this story and always imagined
myself digging in and immersing myself into the writing
process. Well, my world didn't cooperate and the time
to put this book to paper came at one of the most
chaotic moments of my life. This story of my heart
could not have happened without the critiquing,
proofreading and hand-holding from five very dear
people. My heartfelt thanks to my friends Joanne Rock,
Stephanie Newton and Karen Tucker, to my sister
Julie Morrison, and to my husband, Rob. I love you all!

Prologue

Five Years Ago: Randolph Air Force Base, Texas

Lieutenant Nola Seabrook accepted that she could face death on Monday. But for the weekend, she intended to celebrate life to the fullest.

She gripped the door of the Officer's Club bar, preparing herself to do something she'd never even considered before. She intended to find a man—a stranger—for a one-night stand.

Lucky for her, she was away from her home base, which gave her a wealth of unfamiliar faces to peruse. Country music and the clang of the bell over the bar swelled as she swung the door wider to reveal the Friday-night crowd.

No crying. No fear. She would forget herself with some stranger and lose herself in sensations she might never feel again.

Nola shouldered deeper into the press of bodies. The room reverberated with cheering. The place was packed, as she would expect on a Friday night, but the majority clustered in a circle to the side, was the source of the *whoop, whoop, whoop*. And "Go, Lurch! Go, Lurch!"

Lurch? Now there was a call sign for a guy worth investigating.

Curiosity nipped, sucking her feet sideways.

She angled toward the commotion. Sidestepping an amorous couple making tracks toward the door, she caught sight of a chalkboard mounted on an easel. A bartender stood beside with a stubby piece of chalk to scratch out numbers. Ah. Bets. But what for?

She sidled through to the inner circle. Her eyes homed in on the source of the noise. The focus of the cheering was…

A man.

Holy cow, what a *man*. On the floor pumping push-ups in BDU pants and a brown T-shirt, he clapped between counts—ninety-five at the moment. The number hit a hundred and still he didn't stop or even hesitate. Must be his size that earned him the nickname "Lurch" because, holy cow, he was *big*.

Two men in similar uniforms split from the crowd carrying a fifty-some-odd-year-old waitress on their shoulders like Cleopatra. With ceremonial hoopla, they placed her on the man's back. His arms strained against the T-shirt, muscles bulging, veins rippling along the stretch of tendons, but still he pushed.

Up. Down. Again and again.

Ohmigod, her own tummy did a flip of attraction. Arousal. And hadn't she come here for just this reason?

Twenty-five years old and she didn't have anyone else to turn to for comfort, which could really pitch her into a tailspin if she let herself think on it for too long.

Her elderly parents gone. Her marriage kaput because her ex-husband couldn't take the stress of a wife who might not live to see thirty. Zero siblings. Her best friend deployed to Turkey. Her only other friends a bunch of rowdy Air Force crew dogs who spent as much time on the road as she did, and she really couldn't see herself showing weakness by bawling her eyes out to any of them.

Charge ahead, girl.

She made a quick check of his left hand. No wedding band. No pale cheater mark along his tan ring finger. Sheesh, she wished she'd thought to change into something other than her flight suit.

Too late for regrets. She was here now, and if she left to change, the man in front of her might be gone by the time she returned. Besides, she didn't want to miss a second of this display.

Sweat started to pop along his forehead and even a hint along his shoulders, but still he kept moving. The man was a poster boy for health and vitality.

Invincibility, perhaps? All things she so desperately wanted to soak up right now. She found herself clapping the count along with everyone else.

"One hundred forty-eight."

He switched to one-handed push-ups. The crowd roared louder.

"One hundred forty-nine. One hundred-fifty."

He reached behind to steady the waitress and jumped to his feet, easing the apron-clad lady to hers, as well. With all the showmanship of his single-handed display, he wrapped an arm around the waitress's waist, dipped her and gave her a quick kiss before setting her free. "Thank you much, Delphine."

"No problem for you, Captain Rick. Anytime you're in town."

Rick. She liked that name. Solid.

However if she didn't get her butt in gear and make a move soon, he would be gone. Nola stepped forward. And thank you, Jesus, that's all it took.

He looked her way and his deep chocolate eyes held. Without breaking the stare, he smiled, snagged the rest of his uniform off the back of a chair and slid his arms through, slowly buttoning up over his chest.

DeMassi was stitched over the left pocket and above that she recognized the insignia for a pararescueman. He hurtled himself out of planes. Penetrated the most hostile of territories. Anything to save a downed airman, to bring someone like her home.

Honorable to the core and darn near invincible, for sure. Even his patch proclaimed That Others May Live.

He fastened the last button and started toward her. "Hello, Lieutenant Seabrook."

"Hello to you, Captain DeMassi."

"Do you have a first name?"

"Nola, like New Orleans."

"Ah, classy." He extended his broad hand toward her. "I'm—"

"Rick. I heard from your cheering section."

"We're all away from home, coming in from maneuvers to one of our favorite Officer's Clubs, needing to let off some steam. They would have cheered on anybody."

"So you say." She folded his hand in hers, warm and strong.

More of that vitality she needed. Her imagination skipped ahead to thoughts of his hand against her skin. She didn't need to worry about concerns of compatibility or depth. This was about the moment. She refused to let echoes of her mother's preaching voice make her feel guilty or shallow.

Nola's hand stayed connected to Rick's, shaking, seesawing slower and slower, up and down like his push-ups until finally she inched away with a self-conscious laugh, wiping her hand against her flight suit leg. "This is awkward."

"Why so?"

"I want to be all collected and say something femme fatale perfect but now I'm..." She started to turn, her nerve wobbling. "Forget it."

His hand fell on her shoulder, heavy and warm sparking another jolt of that *alive* feeling she needed.

"Wait," he said.

She looked back and what she saw in his eyes mirrored the sensations zipping through her like lightning traveling through an aircraft—not fatal, but hair crackling, unsettling, and oh so invigorating.

"Yes?" She meant the word as a statement as well as a question.

"How about this?" He held her with those deep eyes rather than his hands, as if sensing she needed space. Would he be this perceptive in bed? "Let's not worry about saying the right things. We can say whatever we want, even if it's a damn awful first date wrong thing to say."

Date? She was thinking encounter, but okay. Breathe. His game had intriguing merit. The bar patrons kept their distance, even if they watched with half-veiled interest.

Hesitantly, she hitched her elbows back onto the bar. "You go first."

He propped one arm beside her and leaned in to

make his move, his shoulders blocking everything but him.

"I live with my parents." He thumped his chest with his fist and belched. "Mom does my laundry."

She burst out laughing. Settling a somber expression, she responded, "Speaking of laundry, I just don't get what all the hoopla is about fancy underwear."

"Ouch. You go right for the jugular, lady." He grabbed his head in mock agony. "All right, time for the big guns. My doc said not to worry. It's only a cold sore."

"Then you should be able to enjoy our meal together." She reached for the laminated menu wedged between the condiments. "What's the most expensive item featured?"

"I don't know, but it doesn't matter since I maxed out all my credit cards."

"Fair enough, since it will soon be our money because I'm husband hunting." Nothing could be further from the truth. Her divorce left her scathed, but good.

"Ah, good one." He tapped his forehead, then snapped his fingers. "As long as you don't mind going a lifetime unsatisfied in bed."

"As long as we get to go to bed together."

"I'm counting on it."

She froze and so did he. They weren't playing anymore.

He held out his hand. "Dance with me."

And she did. Silently. Talking softly about anything, mostly seductive. For hours until the crowd thinned and the bell rang for last call. They broke apart and he extended his hand again. She knew if she took it this time they would be heading for a different kind of dance, the one she had come here searching for.

Again, her hand fit perfectly in his. A short stroll later they had walked to his room in the visiting officer's quarters. He kicked the door closed behind him.

She didn't even bother telling him she'd never done anything like this before. Truth or not, she didn't want to sound trite and she didn't intend to see him again anyway. He seemed okay with that. No guilt for either of them. She was through with words and he seemed to feel the same way.

Between kisses, their clothes fell away until only their underwear remained. Skin to skin. Her hands explored the hardened expanse of his muscles more impressive than she'd even imagined.

And her imagination had been mighty darn amazing. She'd been right to do this. This was exactly the escape she needed this weekend to take her away from the ordeal that awaited her next week.

His talented hands made fast work of the front clasp on her bra and he swept the lacy scrap down her shoulders with reverent fingers. A long, slow exhale slid from his mouth, blowing an appreciative whistle over her exposed skin. "Wow, lady, you are something to behold."

Gulping back emotion, she lifted his hand, placed the callused warmth over her bared breast and savored the sensation as if for the last time. Which it very well could be.

Because Monday, combat veteran that she was, she began her toughest battle ever—one that started not with a mission briefing, but with a mastectomy.

Chapter 1

Major Rick DeMassi forced his steel-pin-filled legs to move as he gripped the metal bars for balance. He narrowed his focus to a tunnel as he always did on missions, and no undertaking had been more important than getting back on his feet again.

Every day in rehab he resolved to end this one better than he finished his final assignment during the cleanup after Hurricane Katrina. The carnage had threatened to suck him under, but he'd kept his eyes on the teddy bear ahead, sticking halfway out of the muck. After years of search and rescue, he'd known in his gut there was a child close by.

Too bad his gut couldn't tell him if that child was alive or dead.

Now there weren't teddy bears to zero in on, even theoretically. His teenage daughter was long past the age of such toys. Still he wanted to greet her on his own two feet someday soon—as the hero she thought he was. So he went through the daily torture of grabbing these damn bars and shuffling one shattered leg in front of the other.

What a joke in comparison to the old days when he leaped from helicopters. Swam churning waters. Or sludged through unstable wreckage toward a stuffed toy to pull out a child.

"Careful, sir." The voice echoed in his head. Then or now, he wasn't sure. The stench of antiseptic burned his nose as strongly as the stench of rotting muck. "Steady is better than fast."

One foot in front of the other.

Step.

Step.

Step.

For the kid. For his child. For the trapped child. Both merged in his head. The past and the present. Both times painful, squeezing labored breaths from his body until he thought he didn't have anything left inside him but somehow he kept going. Running then. Shuffling now. The irony didn't escape him, but he wasn't a quitter.

"There isn't much time left," the sergeant said, an orderly watching him like a babysitter in case he fell, but the voice could have been from the past, rushing him along. Urging him to the cargo plane. But he couldn't leave the little girl and her doll behind.

He'd been a crap father to his daughter, always on the job, barely a presence in her life. He wouldn't let this wounded little girl down, too. Even if the best he could do was recover her dead body for burial...

Rick gritted his teeth. "Five more minutes, Sergeant, and I'll be done."

"Roger that, Major."

He would reach the end of this walk without falling. Not like before.

Step.

Step.

Pain. Penance. Step. The sound of airplane engines had hummed in the background much the same as the heater now. Gusting wind over him. The antiseptic scent of the hospital as unwelcome a stench as the stench of...worse than muck...

Death.

Except the child had been alive, even if barely. He'd seen the doll flutter as if tugged.

Walk now. Run then.

He'd pulled the girl out, a child maybe four. They'd

even made it to the emergency personnel where he'd passed her off…just as rotten boards gave way underneath him.

Agonizing pain razored through him. The ground sucked him in. Nails and boards cut into skin and muscle. Bones snapped. Wood tore into his legs. Ripped tendons.

Reach up. Out. Trudge. Don't give up.

His vision tightened the tunnel until he could swear he saw the load ramp at the end of his metal bars. How damn ridiculous was that? Maybe it was just some of that visionary crap the shrink was always telling him about.

Picture what you want. Yeah. That was it. He wanted his job back.

Hell, he wanted his life back.

Okay, the load ramp gaping at the back of the airplane. Go with that image. Move toward it.

Light faded and blazed as he struggled with consciousness. A voice tugged at him from his past. He blinked, cleared his vision and his eyes agreed with his ears. What the…?

He must be delusional thinking of that woman who'd left his bed with only a terse little note five years ago.

Still he couldn't stop himself from croaking out the name. "Nola?"

The woman moved toward him, stepping into the light streaming through the rehab area's windows and revealing a face from the past he'd never expected to see again...

At a time when he very likely didn't have a future.

Putting the past to rest so she could move forward with her future was easier said than done. But Nola was a determined lady.

She needed to wrap her brain around a reality she barely dared dream was real. She'd reached her five-year remission mark.

Her docs all encouraged her to celebrate. The mind and body worked in synch after all.

Easier said than done. Believing in the future was tough after so long of living for today. Milk the most from each second because today was a gift and tomorrow an unknown. Walk to the towering man inching slowly her way.

Her hand closed around her purse, which held her very organized day planner, which held her list.

The list. A list of all the people she needed to make contact with for closure. She'd already contacted every friend she could think of that she may have wronged. A flight student she'd been unnecessarily harsh to during a check ride because in her early days as an instructor perhaps she'd been a bit full of herself.

She'd even contacted a guy from junior high who she'd picked on unmercifully all because she'd liked him and had been too immature to know how to show it. He'd thought she was nuts for calling, but ah well, such was life. She wasn't as worried about looking cool these days.

Today she'd finally tracked down Rick DeMassi, the man she'd left high and dry and gloriously naked in a VOQ room. Once she'd learned of his injuries, her relief at finding him alive had been stronger than she would have expected for someone she'd only spent thirty hours with five years ago. But they'd been a crucial thirty hours. He'd given her a great gift over that weekend, even if he hadn't known.

His talented touch had been the last she'd felt on her breasts. More importantly, his gentleness and strength had bolstered her to walk into hell alone and she would never forget him.

She'd had a mastectomy, but beaten the cancer. Now she needed to see Rick one more time to complete her list before she could close the door on the recovery part of her cancer journey.

So she'd driven all the way from her home base in Charleston, South Carolina, and here she stood at a physical rehab center connected to the same hospital where she'd started her treatments. How ironic was that? But somehow serendipitous.

How bad must his injuries have been for him to still be recovering a year later? Her stomach knotted at even the mention of hospitals. Walking into one usually had her fighting back an anxiety attack. Striding into this one in particular threatened a flat KO.

But she refused to let anything stop her, especially once she'd heard *he* was the patient. No way could she turn her back until she was certain he had everything he needed. Theirs may have only been a weekend together where he unwittingly gave her comfort, but those two days stayed with her still. His face on the back of her eyelids, recalling his touch to override pain…

All of it carried her through hell as surely as his arms had carried her across a room to rest her so gently, seductively on a mattress.

Right now, he could barely carry himself across the room.

Overall, he might be slimmer, but his chest bore the same rippled muscles, his eyes the same fathomless intensity. But his face had an angular cut to it, his features a hard enigmatic look. No joking this go-round as he shuffled the last two feet between them to stop. She'd seen his lips move with a muffled whisper, but couldn't hear what he'd said.

She inhaled deeper with a bracing breath and noticed something else familiar. Even through the antiseptic hospital smell she recognized the spicy scent of him.

A cleared throat pulled her out of her reverie. The sergeant—a therapist of some sort—raised a brow, mumbled something about break time and draped a hand towel around Rick's neck before leaving.

Okey doke. Time to quit daydreaming.

"Hello." She forced a smile over her lips when she really just wanted to stare awhile longer, and doggone it, there went her mother's voice again about rude manners. "I don't know if you remember—"

Long lashes swept down over his chocolate brown eyes and up again in his first sign that he'd actually noticed her. "You're a memorable lady, Nola."

Thank God, thank God, *thank God* he remembered her name and she hadn't just made a total idiot out of herself.

Then a smile twitched at one corner, just a hint but enough of the man she'd known to help her relax her grip on the Tupperware container she'd forgotten she held.

"Why thank you, Rick."

"And you're here because?" He released one bar and held on single-handed.

He looked more "okay" that way. She couldn't gauge the extent of the injury to his legs since he wore dark blue sweatpants and a gray T-shirt with Air Force logos imprinted. Whether or not his sudden easy stance was an act for her benefit she didn't know, but it eased some of the tension inside her. She understood about "brave front" acts.

"I have a list." She blurted.

Sheesh. She was a mature woman. A seasoned combat veteran, trained to fly multimillion-dollar cargo jets and here she was acting like hormonal mush.

All right. Maybe not hormonal. More like knocked

off balance by the whole hospital scene and seeing his pain. Remembering her own. Knowing how pride hurt more than any needles.

Rick shifted from one foot to the other and studied her through narrowed eyes. "They took me off the painkillers a long time ago, so my brain's clear. Still, you'll need to run that by me again, because you're not making a bit of sense."

She couldn't help but notice how he continued to grip the bar, his arm not even shaking, but his complexion beginning to pale beneath his tan.

More of that pride.

She scanned quickly for one of those industrial-looking uncomfy sofas they always had everywhere in places like this, and sure enough there was one right behind her. She plunked down to sit and hoped Rick would cut himself some slack and do the same.

"I was in town, heard through the grapevine that you were here and thought I would stop in to say hi for old time's sake." She lifted the aqua-and-white Tupperware container full of chocolate chip M&M's cookies, raising it at just the right level where he would have to come to the sofa if he wanted a chance at a cookie. She hadn't met a male yet who could say no to cookies. "Hospital food usually sucks, so I figured you might like this."

Actually, she didn't recall much about the hospital food since she hadn't been able to keep anything down during chemo. But every man she'd met worshipped food, so she'd figured cookies would be a decent icebreaker.

Rick shuffled with studied practice—holy guacamole, this guy had pride by the buckets—until he dropped down beside her. Sweat dotted his upper lip but somehow he managed not to sigh when he sat.

"Thanks, you're right." He took the cookies, brow furrowing. "This is still…uh…unexpected."

"I imagine so." She knotted her fingers in her lap, wishing she had that container back so her hands wouldn't feel so empty.

"I should let you get back to work." He nodded to her flight suit.

"I'm done for the day." She didn't want to reference her own swing by the hospital to gather old lingering paperwork and say farewells to some remaining staff members. "What about you?"

"Me, too, but then I'm stuck here. Don't you need to head home?"

"Nope."

"No boyfriend or husband to call?"

"God, no." Her eyes fell to his ring finger. Still bare. Her stomach did that little flip again. "Do you really think I would bring cookies to a guy if I had a boyfriend or, heaven forbid, a husband?"

"Why 'heaven forbid'?"

Her ex shouldn't still have the power to hurt her. She didn't love the bastard anymore. But still, his defection when she'd needed him most cut deeper than any surgeon's knife. "Been there, done that, got the scars and divorce papers to show for it."

"Ah—" he popped open the container of cookies "—so you're a card-carrying member of the Marriage Sucks Club, too, huh?" He shoved a cookie in his mouth and offered her one, as well.

"You could say that." She selected a cookie and weighed her words and finally asked the question that had been nibbling at the edges of her mind the same way she nipped around the cookie. "Want to tell me what happened with the legs?"

He swallowed his treat. "Hurricane Katrina clean-up was hazardous."

The simple words painted a vivid picture. "I'm sorry."

Nola could also tell from his stony face the subject was closed. She understood the reticence well and had to respect the boundaries.

She should probably pack up and go—cookies delivered. Mission accomplished. Page turned and book closed. Except… She couldn't make herself get up off the uncomfy sofa.

"When do you get sprung from this place?"

"Soon."

"You're such a crummy liar."

He shrugged. "I really am out soon. I just have to hire a babysitter and then they'll cut me loose."

"I take it from your tone you don't think you need one."

"Don't want one."

Awkward silence settled, kind of like that first meeting, but they'd already exhausted the wrong-first-date topics. She reached for her purse beside her. "I should go and let you get a shower or something."

Shower? *Sooo* not a memory from the past she needed right now with him all sweaty and hot beside her, with her going on five years of abstinence, with his touch the last she'd felt. She clenched her fists to keep her hand from protectively covering her scarred breast. Yes, she'd had reconstruction, but she wasn't the same by any stretch.

Stop. She wasn't going there today. Except how could she not?

Ah hell, this was gonna be a long night with more than likely a few tears. She was human and closing this book was hard.

Rick grabbed for his crutches at the end of the bars and nodded for the sergeant to pick up the cookies. "I'll walk with you to the door."

She started to tell him no need to bother but then thought of that prickly male ego and opted to keep her yap closed. Let him do what he pleased. She stayed silent while he worked his way to his feet, shuffling to reach for crutches in what must have been a painful maneuver, yet he never even winced.

He nodded toward the hallway and began thumping his way down the hall alongside her. The awkward silence grew heavier with each step down the hall closer to the door. The crisp November air outside along with the bright sun did nothing to lighten the moment.

"Thanks for the cookies."

He cocked his head to the side, quizzical. Not rude enough to glance back at the rehab clinic, but she could sense his itchiness for her to leave.

What had she expected? A resurrection of the relationship? The attraction was still there, but Rick's walls were high. More of that pride. He undoubtedly just wanted to get her in her car and return to his room without falling on his face. The longer she waited, the harder she made things for him.

She needed to quit being selfish. "I know it seems strange, my showing up like this out of the blue. I probably should have called first."

She'd most definitely been selfish, because she'd feared if she'd called first he might have rejected the notion of her coming. God, she didn't like what that said about her. Asserting her needs above the needs or wants of others.

Damn.

He stared at her for a whole cycle on the red light before shaking his head. "I gave up trying to understand women a long time ago. You did a nice thing coming here today for whatever reason. It doesn't have to be complicated."

She could see the strain of standing so long etched on his face, the color seeping away. Yet somehow that took nothing away from his strength, instead only adding to it because of the sheer will it must take to keep his feet under him. She understood well the grit it took to haul yourself through that kind of pain.

Whoa. Hold on. This was getting way too deep.

She backed toward her SUV, fishing in her purse for her keys so she could thumb the remote starter and warm the car. Texas in November wasn't as cold as some of the Northern climates where she'd been stationed, but there was a definite chill in the air. Besides, she always started her car first to get the temperature right.

The weather matched her mood. This hadn't gone at all as she'd expected. She should be happy. Instead she felt chilled.

Hollow.

Nola smiled her farewell to a man she knew she would never forget.

"Goodbye, Rick." Her fingers closed around the keys. She thumbed the remote starter—

And the world blasted into a fireball of heat as her car exploded.

Chapter 2

Blast still ringing in his ears, Rick dropped his crutches and flung his body on top of Nola's. Thank heaven his professional instincts hadn't abandoned him in the rubble of Hurricane Katrina or that flying shard of fender would have caught Nola square on the temple.

He'd lived through his fair share of explosions overseas, but he'd never expected to face one on American soil. What the hell had just happened with Nola's car?

The crackle of flames echoed in his ears, the stench of burning fuel stinging his nose. He stayed on top of Nola while he scanned the parking lot.

No sign of anyone suspicious. Just people with concerned and shocked faces pouring from around the medical park, others running or flattened to the concrete watching. A couple of persons had cell phones in hand, dialing. Good. Cops should be on the way soon.

"Nola?" he asked against her ear, working like hell not to think about how much better her hair smelled after months in a hospital. "Are you all right?"

"I'm okay. Squished, but okay," she gasped. "What about you?"

"Fine," he lied, his left knee already aching like a sonuvabitch.

Nola elbowed him gently in the gut. "Rick? Let me up, please."

"Right." He rolled to the side while still keeping an arm hooked around her waist to anchor her to the ground so she wouldn't do something reckless like spring to her feet. She might be a trained combat vet, but he didn't have any time in the field with her to know anything about her skills. "Sorry about that."

"No need to apologize. Good God, you saved my butt from flying debris." She kept her position, breaths steady as she grappled for her keys a few inches away. "I'm not some prickly ingrate. I just got a little smooshed. You're a big fella."

Not so much as he used to be, but hey, he hated the self-pity gig. No use dwelling on that. Since there didn't seem to be any further immediate threat, time to haul his sorry hide the rest of the way up.

He shifted. His knee hollered back at him.

Damn.

How was he going to get to his feet and keep her safely at his side until the cops arrived? He searched around him for options to brace himself... If he rolled right, he could grab a bench for leverage, pull himself up and sit. From there, he could retrieve a crutch and stand.

Easy. In theory.

Nola reached for her purse from under a park bench and jammed her keys inside. "Do you need help?"

Like hell. "No. I've got it."

"Prideful guy, aren't you?"

"When I fall on my ass you can help me." He reached for the bench and kept his eyes open for surprise threats in spite of the seeming calm after the storm. Screw worrying about himself. Her safety had to be his first priority. "Until then, I've got it. How about that?"

"Fair enough, big guy."

Deep breath. Thirteen teeth-gritting seconds later—yeah, he counted every one to keep his mind on something other than the grinding pain—he was on his feet again scanning the perimeter. And he damn well waved away the attendant coming toward him with a wheelchair. The smart young goon knew to back off and help somebody else who'd apparently twisted an ankle in the mayhem.

Meanwhile, Rick kept the lone crutch jammed under his arm, enough to hold his balance since the majority of the damage was to his left leg. In some portion of his brain, he heard the rustle behind him of Nola pushing to her feet, too. Good. That meant he truly hadn't hurt her when he'd shoved her to the concrete.

Keeping the crutch tucked securely, he grabbed her wrist and urged her to the safety of the portico of the rehab center, into the anonymity of a cluster of nurses and orderlies in purple scrubs. That should serve as a decent safety net of anonymity for now in case someone was gunning for her and waiting around. Watching.

He continued to scan. Adrenaline surged. Damn, he'd forgotten the rush that compelled his body beyond normal endurance, but he welcomed it now.

Still, what kind of guardian did he make? Well, at least he was one more barrier between her and whoever was trying to blow her up. He had his brain and instincts.

And that brain and those instincts were telling him whatever threat there was to her had passed for the moment.

"Ohmigod, Rick!"

Her voice stalled him.

"What happened to your back?"

Hell. Now that she mentioned it… His back did sting almost as much as his knee.

Her hands skimmed over his shoulder blades. "Something hit you. It looks like you'll need stitches."

The glide of her touch almost made him forget the pain.

"Am I going to bleed to death until I get to the doc?"

She moved to his side, the loose blond curls of her bangs brushing along the top ridges of her furrowed brow. "I don't think so."

"Then it can wait." He exhaled long and slow, his fingers itching to thread through that cap of whispery curls all around her face and pull her to his chest where nobody could hurt her. Except his chest wasn't as invincible as he'd once thought. "Any chance your car was a rental?"

She shook her head, curls dancing. "I wish, but no. That was my car. My totally brand-new, just-off-the-lot SUV I'd bought because of my to-do list."

To-do list? Whatever. Irrelevant really. And along the lines of irrelevant thoughts, he could have sworn her hair was straight before. But then women changed their hair. His ex-wife kept her hair permed on a regular basis. God, his mind was racing a million miles a minute.

"Damn. Sorry about the car being new." He scratched his neck and resisted the urge to reach over to his throbbing back. "That sucks for you."

Sirens whined in the background. The cops undoubtedly, a fire truck, too. With some luck they would have an easy answer, not to mention protection.

"Let's just hope there's some mobster who has a car that looks just like yours, who was supposed to be here today visiting his old infirm relative."

Her nervous laugh didn't reassure him in the least. She had a fatalistic look to her that said she accepted she was the target.

More of that adrenaline pumped, reminding him of missions past, the calling that had urged him to join the Air Force. Everything he'd been and done scrolled through his mind, nudging him, whispering at him to reclaim it all. He heard the cops' siren drone closer and yet he couldn't force himself to relinquish his post guarding her. There was no shaking the inevitable.

Uniformed or not, he was back on duty.

Apparently she had a new watchdog after all.

Rick hadn't left her side except when the cops insisted on a solo interview. They'd acted as if they suspected him of being a stalker boyfriend or something worse.

His growl hadn't done much to further his innocence.

She rolled her eyes. Men. She stopped by *their* uncomfy sofa—or at least that's what she'd started to think of it as from their earlier chitchat in the rehab room. Given that most of the physical therapists had headed off for supper, the place was for the most part deserted except for the occasional health-care professional bustling by, past and away.

She was on her own to get her head together before she said goodbye to Rick once and for all, a more emotional event than she'd expected, what with them almost getting blown up. He could have so easily been injured worse if he'd been standing closer to her car. She could have died if she hadn't bothered to warm up her car with the remote starter.

Her knees folded and she flopped to sit on the couch, her black leather boots thudding on the tile floor.

"Are you okay?" He joined her, the cops having stopped keeping them apart.

"I was just thinking how lucky we both are. What if I'd waited to start the car from inside and you'd been standing beside? God. We both could have died." She swallowed hard.

"Two warriors taken down by a car bomb." He shook his head. "Quite an ignominious end."

"No kidding. Is your back okay?"

He shrugged his shoulders, only wincing a hint as the Air Force PT T-shirt tugged at the blood on his back. "Doc put butterfly bandages on while you were interviewed by the cops."

"I'm so glad you weren't hurt worse because of me." She hated to think about causing him more pain.

"You're certain this was meant for you?"

She might as well be up-front with him. She was surprised he hadn't found out during the interview with the police.

Nola slid her purse from her shoulder, unzipped the leather bag and withdrew a manila envelope. She plopped the envelope onto his lap.

"What's that?"

"Go ahead and open it."

Without answering, he pried apart the metal prongs and poured out a dozen or so sheaves of paper, all black-and-white copies of notes comprised of words clipped from magazines.

"The originals are with the police back in Charleston, South Carolina, where I'm stationed, but I keep these with me at all times in case another comes when I'm on the road so I can show local cops."

She watched while he thumbed through the stack of her stalker's notes about how he was watching her. How he'd seen what she chose at the mall. When he'd noticed the specific date she'd come home from a flight.

An outfit of hers he liked most.

The low hum of life in the hall continued while he read. A cart rattled by. A television squawked and talked and blared laughter. Conversation echoed from the chow hall.

All the while Rick's jaw grew tighter with each Xerox copy before he finally replaced the stack into the envelope. "The explosion's not coincidental."

"I don't think so." She'd kept the notes because the

police instructed her to do so, but she hadn't taken the whole thing too seriously until now. She'd been so certain her training would be enough to protect herself against anything anyone could bring her way.

She hadn't factored in car bombs.

"Jesus, lady. How can you sit there so calmly?"

He thought she was calm? Hah.

She pulled a tight smile. "Trust me, my heart's racing like a newbie pilot during a check ride."

"Have you had other accidents like this?"

"This was the first, actually. Before now, I've only gotten letters. I lead a simple life. Work and more work." Of course he was curious, but she'd answered these questions so many times she wanted to bang her head against a wall. "Believe me, the police and I have both been over and over this. We have no idea."

"What about an ex?"

Was he asking about a boyfriend? "There's none in the picture, and certainly none of the psycho type."

"What about your ex-husband?"

More questions about her love life? She certainly didn't have any romance going on now or anytime recently, and she didn't dare wrap her brain around the notion Rick might be interested in jump-starting their short-lived affair. "Peter Grant and I haven't been together in over five years. I even went back to my maiden name the minute we separated."

Which brought to mind the fact that she and Rick had been together just after her marriage breakup, a timing he apparently noticed, as well. The remembered weekend tingled through her mind, as real as if it had happened yesterday as she stared into his eyes, seeing herself and want reflected.

He blinked slowly, without looking away. "Who else could it be then? Stats show a stalker is usually someone you know."

She shook her head to break the contact more than to negate his statement. "This has to be some bizarre coincidence, a threat meant for somebody else, like your mobster theory. I'm not even home, for heaven's sake. And the letters… I can't even hazard a guess. It has to be some freak, one of those strange people you walk past who decides there's some cosmic connection and reads signs where there are none."

"Whatever his reason, there's a huge leap from letter writing to blowing up your car."

His face went hard, protective, a visage she recognized well from working with these guys on a daily basis. He was in defender mode, and all she could think was that *Rick* had been injured because of her.

She reached to touch his shoulder gingerly. "I'm sorry about your back."

He went stock-still. "It's barely a ding. I'm fine."

"Still, is it okay if I say you've got enough on your plate medically?"

"Not really." He growled. Then gave her a begrudging smile. "But then I guess because of that full plate I barely notice this. Now can we drop the subject of the scratches on my back?"

Her mind winged back to other scratches on his back, ones left by her fingernails, the intensity of their sex wringing responses from her she'd never felt before or after.

Actually, she had no encounters after her surgery at all to go by. Showing her scarred body to a man had been a more difficult hurdle to overcome than she'd expected. She'd found it easier simply to focus on work. There was plenty of work to go around these days with conflicts all over the world.

One day blended into the next until suddenly here she was, five years later after her encounter at the bar with Rick and her mastectomy. Ready to face the rest of her life but suddenly having her foundation blown to bits again—literally.

Rick rubbed along his jaw. "You mentioned telling the police about the letters…" he continued like a dog with a bone.

"Of course. I told the cops at home about the third letter. These are copies."

He stared at her and she stared back, sinking into the moment the way she'd done five years ago during their "say all the wrong things" fun moment and before she knew it her mouth was moving. "I want you to feel free to say no because this could really be dangerous.

But I was thinking it might be in my best interest to have a man living under my roof right now."

The minute the words fell out of her mouth she almost looked over her shoulder to see who'd said them. But yep. She'd been the one to voice the outrageous offer. She had most definitely said the wrong first date thing.

She desperately wanted to call the words back. Some maniac was trying to blow her up and now she'd done more to lure a watchdog of a man into her life? Rick had already been one foot on his way toward following her home. Now she would never shake him loose. She didn't need or want this. She'd meant to say goodbye.

Right?

God. How convenient that there were four pretty walls nearby for her to bang her hard head against. The stalker must have been scaring her more than she'd been willing to admit.

"So, Rick? What do you think about my idea?" Maybe he would say no.

And maybe pigs would fly out of her ears.

He scratched along the back of his neck. "How about run it by me again, because I think my hearing's gone bad."

"Never mind. Forget about it."

"Let me see if I follow. It goes something like this. After over a year in a hospital, I need a babysitter who won't drive me crazy. You're an independent soul, and *I* know you can kick any stalker's butt. But having a man around can give off a first line of defense."

Might as well go with it. "Kind of like having a dog with a loud bark."

He picked at the rubber on the top of his crutch. "I'm not sure whether you're complimenting or insulting me."

"I'm not calling you a Chihuahua if that helps." She grinned for the first time since she'd blurted the impulsive offer. "My garage has been converted into a studio apartment so you would have plenty of privacy. It's a first floor, no stairs to worry about."

Ooops. She could see his back getting up about her mentioning his injuries. Men could so miss the big picture. But then who was she to talk? She couldn't bring herself to be with a man because she was wrapped up in her own self-image.

Time to help the man out. He'd obviously been through hell and she understood the bite of those flames well.

"People profile, and you're a really big guy." Ego stroke time. "A police dog?"

"You're good at the suck-up game." He surprised her with a half smile.

A really surprisingly cute half smile on that rugged big mug of his. She had trouble remembering what she planned to say and that was so not good.

So she grinned right back. She could do this. She was good at putting distance between herself and men, after all, she worked in an almost exclusively male environment. "Just so we're clear, I'm not insinuating that we pick up where we left off five years ago."

His smile went wider than hers. "You mean the point where I woke up in a bed by myself with a letter that said, 'Thanks for a great weekend. Have a nice life.'"

Her smile faded, contrition biting. "The letter wasn't that...uh..."

"Callous?"

"Curt."

"However you want to remember it." He passed the envelope of stalker notes back to her.

"I'm very sorry if I was rude. That was an amazing weekend during a difficult time for me." She gathered up the envelope to her chest and made a stab at backing out of this setup after all. "It was a silly idea that we should move in together. I shouldn't have asked you to put yourself in danger. Forget I said anything. I'm just...I don't know. Shaken up, I guess."

He watched her silently which made her all fidgety when she prided herself on her poise under fire.

She got off the fake leather sofa ASAP before she did something reckless like move close enough to share leg-to-leg body heat with him. "It was good to see you again. Enjoy the cookies."

"Nola."

She backed away, hoping the rental car company

would show up with a temporary vehicle for her soon. She definitely needed to get out of here.

"Nola." His voice swelled to a growl.

Her spine stiffened but her feet kept inching her toward the door.

"Nola, damn it."

She stopped.

"I never said no."

"Oh."

He'd let her babble on just to see what she would say?

Rick nodded toward the window showcasing the burned-out shell of her SUV. "The minute that car blew, you had yourself a new roommate."

Chapter 3

Rick dropped onto the edge of the bed in his empty room, resting his crutches against the nightstand. He'd used up his reserves today walking around with Nola. He'd been on his feet more this afternoon than any day since the accident—and he wasn't a slacker around this place by any standards.

He carried his weight on the rehab circuit. He wanted the hell out. Not just out, but on his own two feet. Whole, back to some kind of productive work. He knew he couldn't return to his pararescue life at Davis-Monthan Air Force Base in Tucson, Arizona. That part of his life was packed up tighter than his furniture in storage.

All of which he would think about later. Right now he had a more immediate goal—finding out what was going on in Nola Seabrook's life.

She was with the cops again while they finished up a few more last-minute details about her vehicle. He didn't like being shuffled away for the second time. Who did they think he was? An overbearing boyfriend in a wife-beater T-shirt? He told them he hadn't seen the woman in five years, but cops didn't have reason to trust what people said.

Might as well make the best of this time alone. He figured he had about a half hour to catch his breath before he would see her. Then they would start to make plans to move in together—strangers who knew what the other looked like naked. Except he didn't look the same anymore.

Regardless, he would be out of this place by morning.

He would be living with a woman for the first time in ten years. Holy hell, he really did need a shrink after all because this was the craziest thing he'd ever done and in his line of work, he'd taken more than a few insane risks. Rick shook his head and focused on practical concerns, rather than perfumed and naked notions of sharing a place with a female.

Practical. Focus. Living at her house would serve a dual purpose. He could provide some extra protection, and he could push himself harder on the rehabilitation path than they allowed him here.

A win-win situation.

His cell phone rang from the table beside him, jerking him back to the present. Scooping it up, he checked the screen...and cursed. Truth was he lived to see that number. Now he didn't know what to say to her.

His kid. His daughter. Not a baby anymore.

At fifteen years old, Lauren had expectations and rightly so. Even at full speed, he hadn't been the best of dads, but at least he'd been someone she could brag about. She deserved that hero father who could do more than hobble in and out of her life. He'd never been much when it came to the emotional quotient—just ask his ex. Still, in the minimal time he'd spent in the States he'd tried his best to do something with his daughter. Camping and hiking. Amusement parks and air shows. Beach surfing marathons.

Now he couldn't do more than write checks.

Hell.

His thumb hovered over the On button...then he pitched the phone on the bed. He would have to speak to Lauren eventually. Now just wasn't the best time, right after he almost had his butt blown up by a car bomb...

Then agreed to move in with a woman he'd slept with five years ago. Talk about another sort of bomb in his life.

The phone jangled again.

He stared as if he could will it to silence, prepared

to wait it out again…but his hand stretched out with a mind of its own and clasped the receiver. Hell, he couldn't ignore her call anymore than he could ignore her baby cry at 2:00 a.m. no matter how many times his ex vowed their kid would never learn to sleep through the night that way.

He thumbed the On button. "Hello, Lauren."

"Hey, Dad." Her familiar voice greeted him through the airwaves along with the sounds of some fast-food joint. She always enjoyed hanging out with friends over a burger after school. "How come you didn't answer before?"

"Sorry, kiddo, I didn't have my phone with me." His head thumped back against the wall as he lied to his child. Guilt sucked.

"You always have your phone with you. I mean, God, like whenever I see you your cell phone is like an extension of your arm."

"Like father, like daughter." He swung his legs up on the bed. Might as well get comfortable. She was chatty like her mother, but damn, he'd missed Lauren's voice so much he wanted to take in every second of this conversation.

"Dad, I'm not that bad."

"Kiddo, I pay your cell phone bill. I've seen the number of text messages."

She giggled over the airwaves at their ritual pseudo-bickering. "I'll try to cut back on the LOL responses."

"Don't sweat it. I'm just ragging you." He held the

phone and wished he could give her more than a few flipping extra text messages. "It's good to hear your voice. But why aren't you using the home phone?"

"I'm at a friend's house for the Thanksgiving week. I wish I could see you, though."

Damn. More of that guilt.

He stared out the window at Nola breaking away from the cops in the parking lot near the greasy spoon across the street. She would be back inside before he knew it. His time with Lauren was short.

"Soon, kiddo.

"Sure. It's just…"

He hated hearing the disappointment in her voice. He loved his kid, but better to make sure she had lower expectations than to let her down. "The job makes it tough for me to get away sometimes, you know that."

"Yeah, yeah, you have important things to do." Her laugh thinned. "You would tell me about them, but then you would have to kill me."

How could he know her laugh thinned? Maybe it was just some weird sentimentality on his part because the cell phone connection was so clear she could have been right here in the room with him as they made more small talk. He asked her about school. Thanksgiving break. Things that didn't mean anything, but he should have already known about.

"Was there anything else you needed, kiddo? Because if not, can we talk later? I have to cut this short." Nola would be back any second now.

"Sure, Dad. Whatever."

He couldn't miss the forced cheer in her voice and wanted to kick himself—not that he could do that much damage with even the better of his bum legs. "I will call later."

"Yeah. Right."

"Goodbye, Lauren, I l—"

She disconnected before he could even finish saying he loved her.

Nola hesitated in Rick's door, hating to pull him out of his reverie as he stared at his closed cell phone cradled in his hand. You'd never know he was injured the way he sprawled on his bed like any other guy lounging at the end of a long day of work. He'd changed into fresh sweatpants and a T-shirt stretching over muscles.

His hand still clutching the cell phone.

Who was Lauren? Not that it should matter to her. Logic told her if he had a serious girlfriend, he would be moving in with that woman rather than Nola.

One weekend five years ago gave her no right to feel jealous.

So why was she standing here with the cookies he'd forgotten in her hand feeling the need to close the door on that part of her life? Had she asked him to move in with her because she had some maniac blowing up things in her life?

Maybe the whole move-in thing had been some

spontaneous goof-up that he already regretted now that the Lauren person had called.

Nola rapped her knuckles on the door, drawing his attention away from the phone and to her. "Did you mean it when you said you were going to move in with me?"

"I never make promises I can't keep." His thumb moved back and forth over the small silver phone.

"Never?" She inched into the room, unable to help noticing how stark it looked for a place he must have lived in for months. Whenever she'd spent even a week in the hospital, she'd brought pictures and a water fountain from home along with her helmet to serve as motivation to recover her health and her life. "It must be tough carrying around that much perfection."

He crossed his feet at the ankles, lounging in bed, a look she remembered as well as the errant twinkle sparking to life in his eyes. "When you have a mouth this big, you have to be right."

Laughter bubbled from her in a surprising burst.

She smiled along with him. How could she not? And what a time to realize she hadn't smiled this much in… She couldn't recall how long. "That ego must be mighty heavy to tote around, too."

"You've spent enough time in the military to know it's important to be able to make decisions quickly in the field. Once committed to the plan of action, see it through."

Except she wondered if he could still be in the military with the injury to his legs. That would have to chew at him. Attitude was so important to recovery. She wondered if she would have even made it without the hope of regaining her place in the cockpit again.

Imagining his pain stole the smile from her face. She set the cookies on his bedside table. What a pitiful offering to someone who'd lost so much.

He popped the lid off and pulled one out, waving for her to have a seat in the leather recliner beside the industrial hospital roller table. "Have you had any more thoughts on who would want to blow you up beyond that mystery stranger?"

She sat, because then he would have an excuse to stay right where he was, all comfy on his bed, not because she wanted to stick around longer. *Hah. Liar.* "I lead a pretty benign life. The only people who want to blow me up are enemies overseas and it's not a personal thing, ya know?"

"Sure." He couldn't stop from asking, "You're absolutely certain your ex-husband's not the stalker type?"

"The last thing my ex wants is to lay eyes on me again. Peter's happily married with a pretty new wife living in Georgia. And yes, that stung for three frozen margaritas, a hangover and a week beyond that before I decided to move on." She took a deep breath. "He has two baby girls and another kid on the way."

"That bites."

She jolted. She hadn't expected sympathy. "Yeah. Far worse than losing the scumbag."

"My mom still seems to think I want updates on my ex's dating life."

"God save us from helpful relatives." Was that plural ex wives? Or just one? She was tempted to ask but that would put them on a more intimate footing before moving in together.

Not wise.

He toasted her with a cookie, chewing down two before he spoke again. "Who knew you were here?"

She bristled. "Are you insinuating I didn't tell the police everything?"

"God, you're a prickly thing. I was just wondering if you held back. Sometimes there are things we think sound silly or unimportant."

Her stiff spine eased. "You're trying to help and I should be grateful. This whole thing just has me wound tight. I'm used to worrying on the job, but damn it, I treasured the safe haven of home to recharge between missions and now this stalker has encroached on that."

"Burnout bites, too, doesn't it?"

Burnout? He had his wires crossed there, but she wasn't going to argue with the man. Better to change the subject. "I'm going to say this one last time. The second I asked you to move in, I regretted it. These are my problems and I won't be able to live with myself if something happens to you because of me."

"Well, like I said before, seems as if we're stuck

with each other. So if you don't mind a stubborn, bum leg bodyguard, I'm ready to sign on for the job. God knows I'd like to get out of this place and the last thing I want is one of the prison warden nurses watching over me 24-7."

"So you think I'm a pushover?"

"Hmm. I guess I don't really know you, do I?"

She swallowed hard against the memory of the things they did know about each other, intimate things that heated the air like the lotion he'd rubbed all over her body the second day they'd made love because one night hadn't been near enough. Leaving him had been more than difficult. She'd wanted more, so much more, but time had run out for her.

Now here they were again. What was he saying? She needed to keep sharp around him or her mind would muddle up and she would do something impulsive like ask him to move in with her.

"I may not know you, but I have decent instincts, and I believe you'll be fair. Plus, you have a day job that will give me some breathing room."

"Breathing room is important to you."

She seemed to give him claustrophobia, because his gaze finally broke with hers, away, out the window to the sky he no longer sailed through, only him and his parachute. She imagined the clouds called to him. That she could well understand because the sky called to her as a pilot. She couldn't imagine having her wings clipped.

Finally, he looked back. "Breathing room is critical. Call it my cave time."

"A man who admits to Cro-Magnon traits?" She stuck a finger in her ear and twisted. "I can't have heard right."

"What can I say? *My* ex made sure I understood myself well."

There he went mentioning the ex again. How recent was the divorce? Did it have anything to do with his injuries? He hadn't been wearing a ring five years ago. Okay, she was thinking way too much about his personal life. "This whole moving in together sounds good, but…"

"You're having second thoughts about my coming to Charleston with you."

"I have some kind of maniac trying to blow me up and the last thing I want is to put somebody else in danger. Damn it. I should have thought this through."

"I've already told you, lady, you can't shake me loose now. If you won't let me in your house, I'll be sleeping in a tent in your yard, and believe me, the cold air and humidity will play hell on the rods in my legs."

In spite of his humor, he was set on a path as steely as the metal in his legs. She could tell he wasn't going to back off. She would just have to hope and pray the police protection around her house would be enough to keep them both safe.

Rick had helped her before, and while it had only taken a couple of days, she couldn't walk away from him while he was in need even if it took longer to help him through his recovery.

As much as she chafed at the idea of playing to the he-man syndrome, she also walked in that world daily. She understood how much more it must chafe at him to have the props kicked out from under him.

Men didn't seem to get the fact their strength came from so much more than catapulting out of airplanes.

All a moot point. Apparently he'd decided his redemption lay in protecting her. And he did need her, too. She owed him for that weekend five years ago. She might not have made it through without the confidence he gave her. So much of her survival depended on the mental.

Something she could give him now.

"All right, roomie. How fast can we spring you from this joint?"

Through the café window, he watched the smoldering remains of her car in the lot, firefighters waiting, their foam caking and crackling like an overbaked meringue. Cops were long gone, having already finished their note taking and investigation.

They never even saw him from his perch in the nearby greasy spoon where he inhaled the scent of frying hamburgers and humanity.

If he wanted Nola Seabrook dead now, she would be six feet under. But he liked the hunt.

She always used her remote starter for her car, so

he'd known she would thumb the button rather than turn the key. The look of shock, the fear on her face when her car exploded had been well worth the risk of planting the device in open daylight. Of course the thrill, the rush, that's what this was all about.

Recapturing what he'd lost.

She *would* die—eventually. He had his timetable, but it would be his. He was in control of his life again. He didn't need his youthful body. He'd learned to dominate with his mind, his brain. Working his way onto the military hospital parking lot had been a rush.

His street-smart wits combined with his warrior-honed skills made him indomitable.

The fun was in the cat-and-mouse game. She owed him for the humiliation she'd caused. She wouldn't get away from him this time.

He started to leave, but reconsidered. He needed to eat after all. What better way to savor this victory than with a meal while he regrouped for the next stage of his battle plan?

Apparently he wasn't the only one watching the rehabilitation center with such interest long past what the burning vehicle warranted. A teenage girl stared at the medical building—the windows, not the SUV. She clutched her cellular phone in her hand, her too-tight jeans slung low on her hips with too many holes in them to be accidental. Why did these youths want to appear poor? He'd been poverty-stricken and it was not fun or trendy.

She pocketed her cellular phone and sidled up to the linoleum counter. "I'd like an application for a waitress job."

The woman behind the cash register shook her head. "We're not looking for any more after-school help."

The girl shoved her hands in her back pockets. "Please, I work really hard and it says right there you need help."

"Don't want no troublemaking teenagers." The woman—Jo Nell, her tag read—folded her arms underneath her well-harnessed breasts.

"I won't cause trouble. Besides, it doesn't look to me like you can be picky." The girl's eyes stayed strong, defiant, but her voice had just a hint of desperation. "How about I work for a trial hour, with no pay? Then you can decide. Looks to me like you've got your hands full with all these gawkers trolling in from that car explosion…"

The man working the griddle leaned into the pass-through window. "Jo Nell, quit your yacking and give the girl a chance. She's right. Orders are coming faster than you're filling them." He pitched a pad and pencil her way before snatching up a spatula again. "Number seven coming up!"

The teenager snatched an apron and hooked it over her neck. "Thanks a million. You won't regret it. I've got hardworking genes."

Tennis shoes squeaking, she wound her way across the room with a single-minded determination that made him grin with memories he had not allowed himself in months.

Pencil poised over her paper she stopped by his table. "Have you decided yet what you'll have?"

"I most definitely have." He folded the menu closed. "What is your name, *chica?*"

"Lauren, and hopefully that'll be on my own name tag at the end of the next hour so I can work here near my dad's hospital."

Once he finished placing his order, he smiled at the innocent child, thinking of his own family he'd lost because of Nola. "Good luck, little Lauren. And be careful in this big city. I would hate for bad luck to visit anyone as lovely as you."

Chapter 4

Eyes gritty from lack of sleep, Nola turned the rental car into her dusty driveway and wondered what Rick would think of her little waterside bungalow on a barrier island outside of Charleston, South Carolina. The headlights sweeping the yard showed nothing disturbed. Her alarm system wasn't blaring. Her nearest neighbor, ex-cop Malcolm Cuvier, had kept the lawn in order and watched out for intruders.

All seemed right in her home at least.

Moonbeams reached across the reedy water to illuminate her yellow clapboard house. One story, two bedrooms, with a long living-kitchen area that overlooked a porch along the bay. Not much space, but then how many square feet did a woman need who never planned to marry or have children?

Car idling, she stretched in the leather seat, only to find Rick...

Asleep?

Some watchdog.

Of course he was still recovering and this had to have been a long day for him, even for a fellow who appeared as vital as he did. They both knew he was around for show more than any actual protection he could provide. That had to grate on him. She remembered well her own frustration with how long it took to get back up to speed with simple tasks like cooking a meal without needing a nap—which then meant reheating the darn meal if the whole thing wasn't ruined by the time she woke up.

Rubbing the back of her neck, she threaded her fingers through her hair and shook it loose, relaxing in her seat and staring at her home through "Rick eyes." What had once seemed a lovely hideaway now appeared dangerously isolated. A few lonely crickets chirped, even this late in November, hearty stock hanging around until Thanksgiving week, but nothing else, no one else, her nearest neighbor a mile away through thick trees filled with Spanish moss.

She would be spending the holiday with a man she barely knew, even given the day spent in the car making small talk. Now she knew what fast food he liked—a Big Mac. And what kind of music he enjoyed—retro rock. Still, in her house out here in the middle of nowhere with no family, no love, she felt…vulnerable.

Nola didn't like that feeling much. The cancer nightmare had been rife with helplessness and while she'd tried her best to hold strong, nobody could make it through something like that without moments—hell, to be honest, much longer than moments—of gut-wrenching tears and fears.

This stalker thing brought those feelings back to the fore at a time when she should have been able to put the whole experience behind her. The bastard trying to scare her may not have harmed her, but he had stolen the beautiful sanctuary of her home.

She'd bought the waterside cottage as a gift to herself once she'd begun to trust remission and wasn't trucking it to the doctor every three minutes for some treatment or another. Solitude became a treasured rarity during that first year, her body out there for every doctor, nurse, aide and student to poke, prod and study.

Hurt.

The pain, the total loss of privacy, the tubes, everything had been beyond imagining. Nothing could have prepared her, and heaven knows she'd read and researched every last detail.

Whoa. Back up. Dump that in the past. She didn't want to go there ever again, especially now. Wasn't seeing Rick again about moving ahead? She could help him even if she couldn't help herself.

"So," Rick's deep voice growled from beside her, "are we gonna sleep in the car or head inside?"

Nola would have jerked clean out of her skin if it weren't for years of military training. She turned the key off and pulled it from the ignition. "I thought you were already asleep."

"Nope. Just watching you through my eyelashes." He straightened with a stretch and yawn, his bulging arms and body filling the confines of the vehicle, a bulk better suited to a larger SUV. "People give away more when they think people aren't looking."

"What did you expect to find out about me from staring?" She hated the whole lab item under a microscope feel. "Sheesh, Rick, you could just ask."

"Right."

She didn't like this at all. What had she given away about herself to this apparently too perceptive man?

He opened the door and hauled himself out by holding on to the door frame, the moon casting shadows down the hard angles of his face. She couldn't help but notice more hollows than before.

Sympathy tweaked, chasing away her own insecurities. "Can I help y—?"

"No." Balancing with seeming ease, he opened the back door and pulled out his crutches, his shoulders blocking the moon and any further chance of reading his expression.

She opened her door and swung her legs out onto the dusty driveway. "Just because someone offers help, you don't have to be rude."

"Sorry." He made his way around the hood. "You're gonna have to overlook my grumpiness sometimes. Habit born from frustration."

"Oh, I'm sorr—"

"Don't apologize." He held up a hand. "That makes the frustration worse. I appreciate that you're a nice sympathetic babe."

"Babe?" She snorted. "Are you trying to get me to kick that crutch out from under your arm?"

He grinned and pointed toward her with said crutch, balancing on the other. "Now that's more like it."

Sighing, she waved for him to follow her and charged toward the garage apartment entrance on the side of her cottage. Why hadn't she taken more time to get to know this guy five years ago? Oh yeah, she'd only wanted him to bang her brains out.

"This is it." Her fingers fisted around the keys. A memory of her car exploding swelled in her mind, closing her throat.

Rick rested a hand on her shoulder. "Flashbacks suck."

"Pretty much." She clenched the keys tighter. "Nothing to do but deal with it."

She didn't question how he knew and understood what she was thinking. They had that career experience in common. The trauma of the car explosion may have happened in the civilian world, but it bore a stark resemblance to the type of event that could have taken place on an Iraqi roadside. They'd all been wound tight to be on the lookout for such things for years now.

Nola fit the key in the garage apartment lock. The door swung wide to a one-room studio. She'd used it for friends to visit—more privacy that way. God, she really was a mess these days, but yeah, she had some personal space issues left to deal with.

"You can move things around if you want."

"I'd like to buy some weights tomorrow, so I can work out." He thumped past, proficient with the crutches. "If you don't mind, I'll move the dining table to the side and put mats there."

"Sounds fine to me. You've still got the bar and stools for meals."

He grunted. "Sofa and TV are fine for mealtime."

Sounded pretty much like her mealtime. How logical it would be to eat together. How logical...enticing...habit forming.

Dangerously addictive. "Do you need help settling in or would you prefer some peace and quiet?"

"I really can manage." He propped his crutches against the wall and walked slowly around the apartment, not running any races, but making his way by unobtrusively holding on to furniture or walls. "They held me back by babying me at that place."

Of course he could manage. Right up until the

point where his legs gave out under him. She would have to figure out pride-saving ways to offer help.

Or just quit asking.

Nola walked outside, popped the trunk, yanked his suitcase and hauled it inside before he could argue. She pitched it on the sectional sofa. The bed in the corner would have been optimal, but she figured it was better to ditch the thing fast.

"Okey doke. You're all set." She pivoted on her heel and was out the door lickety-split, before he could get all uptight and macho again.

"Nola," he called from beside her, sprawled in an iron lawn chair just outside the door.

She spun around, startled to see him sitting there. "Thanks."

"Uh, sure." She stared back, the moon streaking star sparks against his jet-black hair and eyes. "No problem."

"Nola, come here."

Nerves pattered. She tamped them down, tossed her shoulders back and inched closer.

"Yeah?" she asked, stopping toe-to-toe in front of him.

"I figure if there's anyone looking at your new watchdog, we'd better clear up that whole me sleeping in the garage thing and why you carried my luggage. Just to be safe, we want them to believe I have a vested interest in keeping you safe."

Hmm. She hadn't thought about that. She backed away a step from the intensity in his opaque eyes.

Her feet shot out from under her—thanks to slick dew in the mulchy leaves. She'd been so busy worrying about him she hadn't thought about herself falling flat on her own butt on top of him.

Then he folded her into his lap, his arms going around her in unmistakable possessiveness. His face hovered just over hers, his mouth so close. She remembered. Oh yes, she remembered the confidence of his kiss. The way he seemed to know right from the start exactly what she wanted.

He listened to her needs.

His thumb resting on the curve of her breast twitched.

With his face so close to hers she could feel his breath caress her as gently as his hands once had. A simple stretch up on her toes and she could press her lips to his again. Would reality match the memory?

That simple thought was enough to help her pull away. She didn't want to lose the special remembrance that had carried her through. To find out it had somehow been a fantasy could make her lose faith in her recovery. How messed up was that? But she'd fast learned much of the healing process involved the body and mind working in synch.

She simply couldn't risk…*fear*.

Nola scrambled off his lap and gave him a bold once-over. "All right, pal, no more of that. People don't have to think we're dating for you to be a watchdog. And about the lap thing…" She swallowed hard. Harder. Gave up getting rid of the lump and just moved on. "We can rest easy since we've now officially cleared away the wrong thing to do right off."

"Just how we said all the wrong things on that first night in the bar?"

"Exactly. Because anything intimate would be unwise. I'm not in the market for a relationship."

"And I came here to watch out for you—not to watch you."

"You have to know, though, that the attraction is still there. We're only human."

His eyes went harder than the steel of his muscles as he stood. "I don't need a pity f—"

"Whoa. You can stop right there. There's no reason for you to assume that from what I said." Her own voice went as hard as his eyes. She didn't take that kind of crap from anyone. "I don't deserve that kind of garbage tossed my way. I wasn't pitying you and I don't say or do things I don't mean. I also don't give my body away that lightly, thank you very much." She pulled herself upright and braced, in charge. "Besides, you're the last guy I would pity. You seem to be able to hold your own just fine."

He smiled, damn him. "Right when I think you're going to piss me off, you go and say something all sweet and perfect."

Sweet? Sheesh, he was charming.

Ignore. Ignore. Ignore. "I'll be back in a few with some clean sheets. You can make your own bed, though, because I'm not any man's maid."

Spinning away, she held her rigid spine stance even though his wicked smile could deflate a dirigible. Whoa, mama, what had she let herself in for?

Well, hell. She'd sure told him.

The grin Rick hadn't even realized spread across his face dug deeper until next thing he knew he was laughing so hard his legs gave out from under him and he fell on his ass in the iron chair again. Even then, his humor didn't fade. It felt good to be treated like a man instead of a patient. Damn good.

Laughter tapering off, he made his way on aching-like-hell legs back into the garage apartment by holding onto trees and then walls until finally he collapsed on the sectional sofa. Plenty of room to stretch out—he liked it, a couch that wasn't institutional-board hard. Air that smelled "home normal" rather than "hospital antiseptic."

Home normal. What would that be? Regular cleaners? Like Windex and some air freshener. What did women call it…?

Potpourri.

Yeah. Sure enough, over there in the corner he saw a little glass bowl with shreds of red leaves and other leafy stuff.

Man, he was seriously losing it if he was getting all worked up over the smell of glass cleaner and nature shavings. Except each of these items were clues about Nola, a woman he'd moved in with when he'd vowed no way in hell would he ever live with a woman again.

After splitting with his ex-wife, he'd been certain he would live alone forever. Not that he was actually living *with* Nola. Still, here he was learning more about her.

Except he did already know about the way she enjoyed having her breasts stroked and nuzzled while he rocked inside her. *Definitely* not a wise thought to be having after a year without sex.

His brain must be malfunctioning from sex deprivation because now that he thought of it… Damn it. He should have checked her part of the house, not that he would make much of an intimidating watchdog right now. His body was pretty much shot. Better to check on her and go in armed with cops as backup if needed.

He reached for his cell phone and dialed her cell from memory.

She picked up after two rings. "Hello?"

"Are you okay?"

"Rick? Why wouldn't I be? I told you in the yard…"

Ah, so she thought he was referring to the almost kiss. She definitely didn't sound as if she had a stalker at her throat. He exhaled long and hard, his heart slowing to half time. "I wondered if maybe your letter-writing buddy might be around."

"Oh. Uh. Right. No new messages." Rustling sounded in the background, like her feet shuffling, a soda can popping, the refrigerator door closing. "I'm just getting something to drink before I bring your sheets. Hope you don't mind the wait."

He wondered what she was drinking, what it would taste like on her mouth.

"No hurry." He could use a few extra minutes to gather some restraint when it came to seeing her, smelling her. Wanting to touch and taste her. *Back to business, pal.* "We need to come up with a duress word so even if someone dangerous is with you, you can let me know there's a problem."

"You're right." She slurped another sip, the slightly undignified sound kinda endearing because it was...personal? "I should have thought of that. How about milk shake?"

"Milk shake?" Another personal fact. She must have a weakness for them. What flavor? Knowing it was wrong, stupid and definitely unwise, he made a vow to find out her favorite flavor someday.

"Sure. Milk shake. I can work it into a sentence without it sounding weird, but the chances of me ac-cidentally using it are next to nil."

"All right then. Milk shake it is." He held the phone and wondered why he didn't just hang up now. "You'll reset your security system after bringing the sheets? And make sure I have the code?"

"Of course."

"Tomorrow, I'll check the place over more thoroughly."

"It'll be good to have fresh eyes and ideas. The guys at work have been driving me crazy hovering over me. Maybe now they'll back off with the kid gloves and start treating me like an equal again instead of acting like I might break."

The guys at work.

She'd already had watchdogs? So why had she asked a busted up dude like him? For some reason her pride had needed to keep them at a distance. Interesting. He wasn't sure whether to be complimented or insulted. This woman was tough as hell to understand. "Good night, Nola."

"'Night, Rick."

He thumbed the Off button.

Potpourri and pride.

Hell. The more he knew about her, the deeper she trenched into his mind.

He levered himself off the sofa, held on to the kitchen island, braced his other hand against the wall. Yeah, it was the principle of the thing, he would get to that crystal dish without his crutches.

And he did. It hurt, muscles tightening and straining, overworked and yeah, he would pay with a sleepless night, but he made it.

Every day a little more.

Leaning against the counter, he opened a cabinet, picked up her decorative bowl and hid the sweet-smelling junk behind a mixing bowl he was mighty damn certain a dial-a-meal guy like him would never use.

He was here to keep Nola safe, heal his legs and move on once her stalker had been nabbed. Nothing more.

Mind set, he closed the cabinet door on the mixing bowl, potpourri and sweet-smelling temptations.

He was tempted to kill her tonight. Drive his chilly rental car from where it was parked two neighborhoods over. Go to her house, break in and just end it all.

Following her from Texas all the way to South Carolina, he had suppressed the urge to run her off the road so many times. The crippled man would have died with her, but there were often unforeseen casualties in war. Given the man's injuries, he would probably welcome death anyway.

Heaven above, he personally would not want to live with half a body. Half a man. Half a fighter.

The temptation was growing so strong to finish it that finally he needed to put distance between himself and her. Once he had been certain she planned to return home, he had sped ahead, skipping meals in order to reach her house first and leave her a welcome-home gift.

She should be finding it soon. Too bad he would not see her face when she discovered his "gift," but he could not risk staying so close to her house. Oh, he didn't doubt that he could remain unseen, but he did question his ability to keep his hands from around her beautiful, vulnerable neck.

He would simply have to relive the expression on her face when her car had exploded into flames. And about her car... She would need to shop for another soon, which gave him another idea. Oh the ideas of ways to torment her. He definitely wanted to play this out a while longer.

Tap. Tap. Tap.

The rapping on the rental car window startled him from his plans, reminding him of the need to stay sharp. She was a fighter, too, after all. A fighter who'd beaten him once before.

He turned to look and found a local police officer with a flashlight.

Relax. Not Nola.

He rolled down the window. "Is there a problem?"

"Well, sir, vagrancy is against the law around here." The county cop kept the flashlight pointed in his eyes. "If you need somewhere to sleep, you're going to have to move your car someplace else."

"I am not sleeping." Indignation sparked. He was not some vagrant, even if he did plan to sleep here eventually, and yes, he hoped to hang around long enough to catch a distant glimpse of her leaving on some errand. Just a look to carry him through.

"Sir, I have received calls from two concerned neighbors about your vehicle sitting here for the past five hours." The policeman swept his flashlight through the car, inspecting. "Thing is, you have stayed in the car. That's making people uncomfortable."

"Since when is sitting in a car against the law?"

"I need to know your business." The flashlight swung directly back into his eyes, blinding him.

All right. He was wise enough to know when to stop questioning the authority figure. He did not need to be hauled in, especially since Nola had reported his letters to the authorities. He *was* two neighborhoods over, but he did not want them making the connection. In fact, he should line up another rental immediately. "I am going to pull out my wallet now, all right?"

"Okay, now. Take it slow and easy, mister."

"I hear you." He reached with one hand into his back pocket, carefully dodging his concealed Taurus .40 caliber pistol. "Here is my private investigator's license. I am simply watching that house over there to see how long he stays with the lady. Let us just say the man is not her husband."

The police officer lowered the beam to the documents, wide-brimmed hat shadowing his eyes until eventually his shoulders lowered as well. If body language could be believed, apparently he had bought the cover story. "I really don't like people causing trouble, loitering around. Don't make me pull your license."

"I know my rights, and the police can only file a complaint against me. They cannot actually pull it."

"Fair enough. But if I receive any more calls about you…"

"My business should be through tonight." A lie, but he lied well and with a straight face. He would simply have to be more careful about staying hidden.

Perhaps he could even look into renting one of the small places nearby. Except the time seemed to be drawing closer. The hotel would serve his purposes as long as it had wireless access for him to work on his next plan to keep the heat turned up on Nola Seabrook's life.

After dropping off Rick's sheets without lingering, Nola finished her diet drink and tossed the can in the recycling bin back in the main house. She should probably find something to eat, but her stomach still hadn't settled from her car explo—

Oh, hell. Who was she kidding? Her belly was turning loop-de-loops over the fact that she had a man living under her roof again. Didn't matter they weren't sharing a bed. They were sharing shingles.

She'd trusted a near stranger with her safety over a squadron full of friends. How messed up was that? Or maybe it made total sense because this way she maintained some control. Some distance. Not that she'd kept her distance very well when she'd landed in Rick DeMassi's lap earlier. What a freaking mess.

Okay, she would reclaim her life. Be normal.

Nola snagged an apple from a basket on the

counter and crunched. She hit the remote to turn on her favorite jazz music and started shedding clothes on her way to her bedroom.

She thrived on disarray in her home. She had more than enough of regimen at work these days. Her T-shirt went sailing to land on the back of her sofa. Nola kicked one shoe under the dining room table, the other under her telephone table.

And speaking of her phone, she'd better keep her cell phone with her for emergencies. She looped the string holder around her wrist.

"Milk shake. Milk shake. Milk shake." She repeated the duress words a few more times with a dance step to her walk as she committed it to memory.

She unbuttoned her jeans and kicked them into a pool in the hall until she wore only her sport bra, high-cut cotton panties and Christmas-green socks. Back before her cancer, she'd lived in a totally orderly world of beige and white, only to discover she controlled nothing. Now, she lived her life differently, vibrantly, with a certain respect for the psychedelic chaos factor.

Her problem lay in trying to blend the two parts of herself, past and present.

She padded down the narrow hall full of pictures of planes and friends snapped around the world. During her recovery, she'd taken a framing class and matted photos from her past in bright colors. She'd populated her home with the memories to give herself hope of adding more images someday. And she had.

Would she add one of herself with Rick to look at after he left?

Now wasn't that a dangerous thought to carry into her bedroom? She creaked open the door, swinging the cell phone on her wrist, a reminder that Rick was only a simple call and wall away.

Had she been totally reckless to invite him here with their sexual history? Or maybe he was exactly the man to invite under her roof, perhaps under her bedspread, as well. He had scars, too. Could he be the one she could trust to show her own?

All-too-deep thoughts for her exhausted body tonight. She stepped into her room and clicked on the switch for her Tiffany lamp to cast multicolor lights over her Laura Ashley patterned pink-and-white room full of pillows and trinket boxes and her newfound joy in clutter. She soaked in the familiarity of it all, readying to flop into the plump comfort of her bed…

Only to stop short.

Lying on her floral pillow sham rested a surprise box of Godiva chocolates. Which would have been creepy enough by itself, except the box was open with half the candies missing and only the light chocolates remaining, as if someone had removed all the dark.

The kind she didn't like.

Her fingers shook as she reached for her cell phone, already whispering, "Milk shake."

Chapter 5

"**Y**ou can't sleep on a sofa."

Can't? No word stirred Rick to be contrary more than that.

Standing in Nola's living room after the cops had left from taking their statements, he had plenty of frustration built against her candy-leaving stalker as it was. Rick refused to let her boot him out of her place in some misguided sense of independence that was flat-out unsafe.

Nola had to know this ramped things up to a new level of dangerous. She might look unfazed standing there in her sweatpants and T-shirt with her fists perched on her hips. But he still remembered those same fists shaking when he'd seen her in the sport bra and high-cut panties she'd been wearing when he made his way into her place after her "milk shake" call.

This stalker guy had slipped past her security system while she was out of town—and blown up her car in another city. The fella was freaking everywhere at once. Not a chance Rick was letting her out of his sight, even if it meant sleeping on her flowery sofa that oozed estrogen.

He met her nose-to-nose. Okay, more like nose to curly hair. "Like hell I can't sleep there."

"Let's be realistic." Her fists slid from her hips and she backed away to sit on the edge of the matching poofy chair. "You're still recovering from major injuries. There is no way I'm putting you on a sofa, or even a pullout couch."

"And there is no way I'm letting you sleep in this house alone." He wasn't going to be maneuvered through her obvious attempt at low-key body language. "The cops may not have been overly concerned about the private investigator vagrant they mentioned being the only disturbance recently, but I'm not dismissing it so easily."

"It was actually a couple of neighborhoods over," she said, her voice rock solid. "And my neighbor—"

"That Malcolm Cuvier fella, the ex-cop?"

"Yes." He'd been Johnny-on-the-spot when the cops showed up. Forced into retirement at forty when he took a bullet in the lung, he still listened to his police scanner religiously. "He's going to call in some favors and look into it a little deeper for us."

Rick dropped to sit beside her on the arm of the chair. Besides, his legs were aching a little. He wasn't getting all softhearted over this lady. He just needed to take care of his body since she was counting on him.

Still his hand gravitated to rub along her back between her shoulder blades absently while she stared off into space. He thought through what the cops had relayed about the stranger dude nearby. "All right, so the vagrant had an accent and was around fifty and claimed to be a private investigator. Could be our guy or hired by our guy. It's a start, more than we knew before."

"We?" She tipped her face up to his.

"Duh. You asked me to help out, remember?"

"Right." She half smiled. "*Duh.*"

He started to pat her back again only to realize he was still touching her, in fact had been rubbing soothing circles along her back the whole time.

She looked up at him, his head beginning the dip down that would take him to her lips. Already the memory of the feel and fit of her came back to mind a second before he rediscovered... Yeah. He skimmed her mouth with his, his hand palming her back more firmly, drawing her closer. The scent of her filled him, spurring him to take this further, deeper, but what did she want?

He took her little gasp, the tiny moan in the back

of the throat as an affirmation and delved into her mouth. No protest. Definitely no protest. Her hands slid up to his shoulders, around his neck.

Holy crap.

At least she had her clothes on now. He couldn't erase the image of her in those high-cut panties and sport bra, but at least the clothes offered a boundary of sorts or they would both be in serious trouble. Because as much as he was enjoying this kiss, he knew things wouldn't go any further.

He didn't question how he knew their limits when they'd both hopped into bed so quickly before, but somehow, he just knew...call it taking a radar read off the woman. She had a wariness to her now that hadn't been there before, a steeliness too, no question. Nola also had more boundaries, and he had to admit he felt pretty damn much the same.

He couldn't help but notice other differences, too. She was thinner, more whipcord. His mind played tricks on him because he could have sworn he remembered fuller breasts, but still he found her no less attractive. Just different. Like with her new curls.

Of course a lot of years had passed. His memory could well be faulty. His hand fisted in her T-shirt at her waist as he thought of how he'd palmed her breast...

No. Stop. He wouldn't go there in his head and if he didn't pull back from this kiss soon, he would be going much further than either of them was ready for.

He couldn't afford the distraction when he needed

to think about her safety—especially when he had a long night ahead of him sharing a room with her. Easing away, he ended the kiss with a final brush over her lips, then the tip of her nose, her closed eyes, her forehead, before resting his chin on top of her head.

Best to keep things light. They couldn't pretend the kiss didn't happen, but he didn't want to talk it to death. He'd better grab hold of the conversation first.

"About watching over you tonight and the whole couch dilemma, if I sleep in your bed, I think I may suffocate from all the ruffles and powder puff."

She chuckled. "That bad, huh?"

"Nah, just a surprise since I expected something more…sleek. But I like surprises." His smile faded and his hand slid away from her back. He draped his arm along the back of the chair. "Even if I conceded and let you sleep on the sofa, you would be out in the living room while I'm in the next room, down the hall, too far away."

Her spare room only contained office furniture, not even a sofa.

"How about this then," she offered. "We'll both sleep in the garage apartment tonight. You sleep on the bed and I will sleep on the sectional sofa, which does have a pullout sofa bed."

He could live with the compromise. The place had fewer entrances to guard and the guy would actually be less likely to look for her there. Yeah. It fit. She was a reasonable woman. A reasonable woman who'd had one helluva day. He couldn't resist teasing another smile from her.

"On one condition."

She cocked her head to the side. "What would that be?"

"Tomorrow, you let me bench-press you as my weights so I can restore my lost testosterone percentage points."

Her shoulders shook with another laugh, weary, but still a solid chuckle. She extended her hand. "Deal."

"Deal." He closed his fingers around hers—soft, long fingers he could remember stroking over him with tender thoroughness, leaving him damn near begging at times.

He gritted his teeth.

Definitely a long night ahead of him.

God, this was a long flight.

Nola gripped the stick in her hand. She'd been called in to sub for Bronco, who'd thrown out his back in an intramural game of basketball. She'd barely made the requisite twelve-hour crew rest for the afternoon flight, but the squadron commander really needed this mission—with the demo of new upgrades to the aircraft. And, quite frankly, she hadn't minded the space from Rick after spending the night in the same room, after sharing a hair-curling kiss neither of them discussed. Instead, she'd hugged a pillow and listened to him breathe.

Roll over.

Rustle the sheets.

Too many memories stirred of sharing sheets with him.

She'd suspected his legs were bothering him and she'd wished she could offer a massage, but... They couldn't go there, not without things leading further. She needed more time with him before she made a decision about that.

He'd ridden with her today to the base, checked in with the clinic about his rehab and then detailed his own plans to check out her security.

Nola worked her boots against the rudders, slicing the planes wings through clouds. Another ten minutes and they would be on autopilot, so she soaked up these remaining seconds of control, power. Freedom. She loved to fly, had known it was her destiny since the instant she'd sat behind the controls for the first time. Sure she'd started out piloting because she wanted to prove as a woman she could equal any man... Now she flew because she couldn't imagine not flying.

She and her ex-husband had met in flight school, had fallen hard and fast. Their relationship had been based on attraction and shared dreams.... Until Peter had washed out of flight school in the last month.

He'd been one of the lucky ones who could stay in the Air Force. Some who washed out of training didn't even get to stay in the service. Peter hadn't considered himself lucky at all. Losing his dream had changed him. He'd served four more years in the service at a desk job before putting in his papers.

Why was Peter so heavily on her mind today? Had to be because of having a man under her roof again, even if it was purely platonic.

Purely? That kiss had been anything but platonic. If the two of them were already traveling this far and fast down memory lane, they wouldn't last too much longer without making their way to the end of the map. Had this been her reason for tracking him down? She'd chosen him to be her last lover before the operation, did she want him to be her first after surgery, as well?

That scared her witless because the intent would have been subconscious and she liked to think she was making her own choices these days. And what did all of this have to do with her ex and him washing out of pilot training?

More of her flipping subconscious at work.

"What would you do if you couldn't fly anymore?" The words fell out of her mouth of their own volition. Luckily, only her boss flying beside her would hear and not the crew in back.

"Who gave you the grumpies instead of bananas with your Cheerios?" Lieutenant Colonel Carson "Scorch" Hunt glanced up from checking the fuel display.

"Ha-ha. Very funny. Not." Her hand clenched around the stick. She wished she could mask her feelings as well as the clouds hid the ground below. "I'm being serious."

"Is there something wrong?" All humor vanished from his poster-boy-perfect face—she preferred craggy these days. "Oh damn. Is your cancer back?"

"No! Ohmigod, no." Thank heavens. "And I certainly wouldn't tell you in the middle of flying and risk unsettling our concentration."

"Of course. All right." His exhale filled the headset long and slow before he continued, "This is about the man living with you. There are going to be a lot of broken hearts around the squadron once this becomes common knowledge."

How did he already know about Rick liv—? "Are there no secrets in this squadron?"

"Afraid not," he said as he opened his flight bag to pull out his lunch with Beachcombers Bar and Grill stamped across the sack containing a hamburger that smelled too good. "I heard from Bronco that you called his wife since she's a flight surgeon to get her advice on the best options for rehab in the area."

Bronco always had been a big ole gossip. He must have spilled all when he called in sick because of his back. Well, this squadron thrived on practical jokes and Bronco was about to be the recipient of a whopper practical joke except she wasn't feeling particularly funny right now.

"Yes, I have a friend recovering at my place for a while."

"A PJ." A parajumper, also known as a para-rescueman.

"Yes."

"Must be hell."

"Excuse me?"

"Those guys are hard core. He must be going through hell adjusting. You're a good friend to take in somebody carrying that much baggage."

"And you sure are one chatty boss."

A boss she had dated back when their ranks and positions were closer, before he was the head honcho. They'd gone out a couple of times, had fun, but soon realized there simply wasn't any chemistry. The friendship stuck, though.

Scorch turned to face her full on, the plane skimming through a sky as blue as his serious eyes. "Yeah, I get that you want me to back off, but hell, Bronco's a gossip and I'm freaking Ann Landers. So here goes. How did you feel when you thought you wouldn't fly anymore?"

She started to tell him to take a hike, *sir,* and then…she stopped and thought. If she meant to move forward, she had to stop pushing people away. Scorch truly was a good boss who cared about his people. Beyond that, he knew her well as a friend, in fact knew more about her than most folks.

Yet, she'd never told him about Rick.

Still, she could carry on this conversation without relaying that tidbit.

Deep breath. Leap. "I was so wrapped up thinking I might not even live, the notion of losing my wings wasn't up front in my mind."

"Whereas your friend's mortality isn't in question since his isn't a life-threatening illness."

She nodded.

"There's no question that this job of ours is more than a job, a calling, service to country, to others above self. Those PJs really push themselves—That Others May Live."

"Their motto."

"Think about your cancer, how you fought so damn bravely, but all the while preparing yourself to die."

Ah. The clue bird landed on her head. "He has prepared himself to die, but never prepared himself to live."

"And since I'm the boss and know everything, you might want to take those words to heart yourself."

An image flashed to mind of Rick's face as they'd driven around base earlier—the hunger in his eyes as he'd stared out at the flight line at the airplanes. Planes he'd once jumped out of to save lives.

Just as her boss had said. She'd faced the possibility of death. But she'd never thought about living—and losing her dream.

Rick faced that nightmare every day, something far less clear-cut in its healing. How could she have been so dense? Hell, she lived with a man who couldn't face losing his dream. She'd seen how it tore apart her ex-husband watching her put on her flight suit each day.

Rick would help her, but this had to be painful for him in ways he never would have anticipated. And—ouch—that stung her in a way she hadn't foreseen, either.

Self-revelations hurt as much as any incisions. This healing process just went on and on and on. Sheesh, when would she get to just live a normal day?

Maybe this was normal. The good and the bad. Learning and moving ahead. Time to quit grousing and start embracing those lessons so she could live each day a little stronger and wiser before she moved on to the next.

Definitely ouch.

Chapter 6

"So I've finally found your vulnerability," Rick pronounced from the passenger side of the rental SUV, working to inject levity in his tone.

He hurt like hell. The rehab folks here took torture lessons from the same folks as the technicians in Texas. His legs hurt. His head hurt.

And after three nights sharing a room with Nola, other parts of him hurt even worse.

He was grouchy as all get-out and determined not to show it.

"Huh?" Nola glanced from the road to him then back to the street, turning off the interstate.

"Your weakness." He hooked his elbow on the

open window. Tough to believe tomorrow would be Thanksgiving, with temperate weather like this. The time for family dinners. He squelched thoughts of Lauren at two with mashed potatoes all over her chubby cheeks. Patience. "Your tender spot."

"Fat chance. I have no tender spots. I am a warrior woman, invincible." She winked.

"Yeah, right. Okay, warrior woman." Actually, there was something to what she said. She did have training he hadn't given as much thought to as he should. She could fight her stalker, maybe better than he could right now with his exhausted body. God, he needed a nap, but she'd been all psyched up to go car shopping and he wasn't letting her out of the house without him or one of her flyboy buddies.

He shifted in his seat, his legs protesting—loud— at the lack of space. He needed a half hour of Jacuzzi jets massaging his sore muscles. "Aren't you curious as to what I've determined?"

"Do tell." She pulled off the access road into the auto-mall.

"You're scared of car dealers."

"Not hardly." Poorly masking her distaste, she stared at the line of dealerships proclaiming holiday sales, multicolor triangular flags flapping in the wind.

"Then why ask me along?"

Her knuckles went white, her jaw set, she put the car in park. "Because you're supposed to be watching out for me and making this stalker guy think I have a big-ass tenant. And by big-ass, I do mean that you are being an ass today."

"Why thank you, ma'am." He'd forgotten how prickly women could be. Living alone in a cave had its appeal. Well, except for the no sex and soft womanly curves part. "I do believe we may have more in common than we thought."

Her baby-blues eyes went wide. "Did you just insult me?"

"You insulted me first."

"Well, that's mature."

"More and more in common by the second."

That spurred a laugh from her, something he enjoyed doing more and more by the *hour*, enough that it took his mind off his legs for the moment.

"Okay, fine. I brought you along because, yes, it will be easier to work with the car dealer if you're here." She held up one finger, firmly. "I have absolutely no doubt that I could get the same deal on my own, but it would take longer and be far more exhausting than if I just let you two men do your grunt, grunt, bump chests, circle the fire, macho thing."

"All right, now that I'm clear on my role." He cleared his throat. "Ugh."

"Perfect." She gave him a regal nod. "Here are some examples of the car I'm looking for, with my hopeful price listed as well as my absolute top-dollar price."

Nola passed him a flyer insert from the Saturday

paper with three cars circled in red marker, with her notations alongside.

As they made their way to the dealer of her choice, he asked questions concerning loan lengths and payments until he had a firm grasp of what she wanted. He even did his best not to roll his eyes when she specified color—why was car color so important to women? Must be like the potpourri thing. And maybe somewhat like how he hated bargaining while on crutches.

Three haggling hours later, he'd landed the deal she wanted, closer to the wish price than the top-dollar price. All they needed was the bank okay to clear the loan and she could turn in the rental for her spiffy new convertible.

Damn, he felt as if he'd speared the wooly mammoth to haul back to the cave, and double damned if he hadn't forgotten about his aching legs for more than thirty seconds. Not an evolved kind of thought by a long shot, and surely she would laugh and label it another "ugh" moment. Thing was, her laugh would spark another chest-thumping thrill of victory in him.

What was it about this woman? She could take care of herself, manage this on her own and yet here he sat, waiting to help her.

There was…*something* about her.

Something that made him want to share the Jacuzzi with her for more than sex, but with champagne and strawberries while her laughter rolled with the bubbles.

The returning salesperson popped that fantasy faster than any cork.

"Um, Captain Seabrook, I'm afraid there's a problem with your loan application."

Back home, Nola stared at her computer screen with disbelief.

Still, there was no denying what she saw. Her bank account was empty. Her savings account—also zilch. Her credit cards all canceled.

What the hell was going on?

Her fingers hovering over the keyboard, her hands shook as she studied the mess of her financial life.

She spun in the office chair to face Rick in the extra chair beside her. "Any other ideas I might have overlooked?"

He scrubbed a hand over his five o'clock shadow. "You're a computer whiz lady. Appears to me like you've covered every angle here. This guy must be damn good. Still, there's always a path. I'm sure the bank will be able to straighten this out fairly quickly. There are safeguards out there against identity theft."

"And there are nightmare stories about people who never recover from the financial damage." Her throat started to close up as her mind traveled the path of all the bills she had to meet and couldn't...

"Nola, breathe. Think." His hand rubbed along

her back. "This could also be a way to track the person who's been tormenting you."

She sagged back into the wheeled office chair. This totally sucked. "You're right. I just feel so…"

"Violated?"

"Pissed off!" She kicked back from the desk, in need of distance. It would be too easy to move closer to him again and continue to take that comfort.

"Atta girl."

And somehow that distance made things worse because she *wanted* to move closer. This stalker creep had her really on edge. "And yeah, violated, too."

"You have every right."

"My life is so screwed up. This has gotten to the point where they're going to take me off flying status until things are settled. I just know it because what normal person could think straight right now?"

"Quit focusing on what you can't do and let's think about what we can. We can notify the police right away to file a complaint to add to your case. And after Thanksgiving, having the Air Force's OSI—" Office of Special Investigation "—check into things could be a valuable extra civilians don't have."

"I realize that." She hated feeling so under a microscope again. She needed to think about something else—anything else. "Did you get settled in with everything rehab wise here?"

"I only have to go twice a week now. No big deal. The rest is on my own. My disability pay meets the bills, but once we nab this guy of yours, I'm gonna have to start thinking about something to do so I don't go stir-crazy."

She started to ask him what might interest him, but all the memories from her divorce came slamming back down on her. She'd fallen so short of the mark in being supportive for a man she'd claimed to love. How could she be sure she would say the right thing here and now?

And with those kind of thoughts kicking around in her head, the last thing she needed was to dive back in for a repeat of that kiss, no matter how much her body screamed, "Go for it!"

She would stand a better chance at success untangling her messed-up finances.

Rick popped the DVD into Nola's player and hoped the movie would help her think about something tonight other than the ill-fated car shopping spree. Since tomorrow was Thanksgiving, nothing could be done until banks reopened on Friday. And probably nothing would be solved until the following week.

At least they had gotten the report filed with the police to add in with her other information about the stalker.

He wished he could do better for her than supply the turkey and entertainment, but at least he had an ATM card and a full bank account. There hadn't been many movies left at the video store by the time he'd talked her into abandoning the computer and making some Thanksgiving plans. So they'd opted for old mysteries.

Rick commandeered the remote and hit Play, grabbing hold of the chair as he made his way slowly back to the froufy-poofy sofa to sit beside her. "We've got to do something about the size of your TV."

"What's wrong with the size of my television?"

"You need a magnifying glass to see the screen."

"Excuse me," she sniffed, "but twenty-seven inches is plenty respectable. I assume you're one of those wide-screen plasma guys."

He grunted a respectable ugh.

"Now thump your chest. Come on. Give it a good thump along with that grunt."

Rick pitched a handful of popcorn in his mouth and fought back the urge to, to…what? Kiss her again? No. More than that he wanted to charge out of here and set things right for her. Instead, he was stuck watching freaking movies and eating chestnut stuffing for the next thirty-six or so hours. But then, keeping her calm had to count for something.

Damn. He was now *her* babysitter.

She had to hate that as much as he'd hated having sitters. Must be the holiday making him so morbid. And the phone call he had to make.

He looked forward to talking to his daughter…and he didn't. He would have to lie. That was never fun.

Not much longer, he promised himself.

"Quarter for 'em." Nola's voice cut through.

"What?" he asked.

"Quarter for your thoughts. I figured a penny would only buy me a grunt, what with the way prices have gone up and such. So I hedged my bets with a twenty-five cent request."

He couldn't think of a reason not to tell her. "I have a daughter."

Her pretty blue eyes blinked fast. She seemed surprised. "Oh, I imagine I should have guessed... There's no reason I shouldn't have... Um, oh. Anyhow. How old is she?"

"Fifteen."

"Do you have a picture?"

He pulled his wallet from his back jeans pocket and flipped it open to one of Lauren a year ago. Poor kid looked like him. He thought she was perfect and knew she would grow into a stunning woman, but his ex had let him know all about Lauren's self-image struggles—which always translated into requests for more money for a beauty treatment or clothes to make Lauren feel better about herself.

He thought backing off and letting the kid be a kid would make her feel better. But what did he know?

"You're going to have to beat the boys off with a stick," Nola proclaimed and won a piece of his heart for seeing his kid the way he did.

How interesting that Nola could see what Lauren's own mother couldn't. "Not as effective as I used to be with the intimidation factor, but yeah, I think I can keep my daughter safe."

Or he intended to be able to soon. Focus, dude. Focus.

She passed his wallet back. "You must have been young when you had her."

"Lindsay and I got married right out of high school." He tucked the folded leather into his back jeans pocket and tried not to think about the fact that he'd added a condom to his wallet again this past week.

"You worked through college?"

"Both of us did. It wasn't easy." Not by a long shot. But they'd had a lot in common then, same background and family friends. He still didn't understand what had gone wrong, other than too much time apart. And if he couldn't understand, then how could he try again? Damn. "We knew the odds were against us from the start. Then the TDYs piled on and Lindsay met someone else. I'd seen it happen so many times to my pals and still I was surprised."

"And hurt."

Only a robot wouldn't be hurt when a marriage fell apart and as much as he tried to keep his feelings in check, he was far from robotic.

"I'm sorry if I overstepped there. I've been in the divorce war trenches… Well, I'm sorry."

"No need. We stopped loving each other a long time ago."

She peered down into the bowl as if searching for

answers under the pile of popcorn. Finally, she spoke again. "So tell me more about your daughter."

He was embarrassed to admit how little he knew about Lauren. He vowed to make things better… except he'd been vowing that for a long time. Another example of how he sucked at relationships.

Nola looked up from the bowl. "Is that sacred territory, too?"

"We don't get to see each other all that often."

Her pretty arched brows rose.

"You disapprove." And who did she think she was to pass judgment?

"It's not for me to say. I don't know your life. I'm not a parent."

Damn straight. Except she was right.

"But you obviously have an opinion."

"I'm of the opinion that you are hogging the bowl of popcorn. Pass it over or pay the fine."

"The fine?" Thank God they'd left the other discussion behind.

"You'll be doing the dishes for the rest of the week."

"I'm recovering from serious injuries."

"You seem totally able-bodied to me."

He snitched the bowl from her lap. "Tyrant."

"Popcorn hog."

He scooped kernels up and brought two to her lips. Slowly, she opened and let him feed her. Holy crap. He recognized an invitation when he saw one.

While she chewed, he kept his fingers against

her lips, his eyes locked on hers. Less than a week and they were already getting this close. There was no question that they were headed for naked pretty soon. If not tonight, then sometime in the very near future.

He wasn't sure about the wariness in her eyes. Because of the stalker maybe? Hell, he would just have to dig deep for sensitivity and ask. Maybe he would kiss her first and knock down a few more walls and years between them.

As soon as he formed the thought, a ringing jarred him out of the sensual haze.

Her phone?

No. His cell. Rick blinked fast twice. He reached into his pocket for his cell phone. He glanced at the faceplate…Lauren.

"I'm sorry, Nola." He shuffled the bowl of popcorn to the coffee table. "I really have to take this call."

"It's okay. Please, go ahead." She hit Pause on the remote and grabbed the bowl on her way off the sofa and toward the kitchen. "I'll make more popcorn."

Fear. He saw flat-out fear in the woman's eyes as she backed away from him. He'd been in combat with enough people to recognize the emotion when confronted with it.

What had happened to her during the past five years? And why was she so frightened of him, a man she'd known all of a few days?

A few very intense days and sexual nights.

He could only deal with one crisis at a time, starting with the one in his hand. "Yeah, hello, Lauren. Happy Thanksgiving, kiddo."

Chapter 7

Lauren? Who was Lauren?

Wait. Nola stomped down the initial flash of jealousy she had no business feeling after knowing this man only a few days and thought through the snippets of conversation she couldn't help but overhear. She forced her feet to keep on carrying her across the living room, through the dining area toward the kitchen.

He had called Lauren "kiddo." This must be the daughter he mentioned.

Emotions tangled in Nola's stomach like two silver dog tag chains clenched too tightly in a fist. Her feet slowing, she willed her stomach to settle and worked to untwine the emotions so she could understand her feelings.

She'd learned the benefit of exploring the causes behind emotions during the darkest months of battle with her disease. Sometimes the process of digging for root causes only unearthed stark fears she couldn't help. But other times, she'd excavated more tangible concerns that she could combat on a concrete level.

Struggling to recapture the tactic, she realized that relief emerged first, an obvious reaction. Rick wasn't speaking to another woman. She didn't have a claim or right to feel that way, but emotions weren't logical. So there.

And then? The next silver chain… Far more intricate.

He had a child with his ex-wife. Nola pressed a hand to her stomach, less clenched but totally churning. She'd come to peace—at least somewhat—with the fact that she wouldn't have children. Her insides had been so fried from the radiation. She could have had eggs frozen and stored…she'd considered it, and finally been too emotional to make any more decisions.

She'd been certain she wouldn't marry again. Even facing life had been more than she could envision and if—a big if, that scared her to even consider—if she lived, a career was all she could consider.

So here she stood, with her career rock solid and

a hot man in her house, a man who attracted her big-time. Yet she couldn't bring herself to make a move for something she obviously wanted.

Sheesh. She'd faced combat in Iraq. Even been taken prisoner by an arms dealer during a mission gone rogue in South America. Still, here she was running from a man she'd already had wild monkey sex with, just because he might give her a warm wonderful kiss tasting of butter and blessed promise.

"Lauren?" His voice drifted from the other room. "Are you sure everything's okay?"

Nola hooked her shaking fingers in her back pockets. The kid deal definitely freaked her out. He was a father. That put him in a new light, one that scared her. Why, she didn't know since she didn't want long-term.

Good golly, what a mess she made.

He cupped his hand over the phone. "Nola, could we put our conversation on hold for a few? It's my daughter, Lauren."

Uh-oh. She hadn't realized she still stood in the kitchen doorway and he must want privacy. She'd thought she'd left. Yipes. This guy robbed her of awareness of her surroundings, a spooky thought for an independent woman who prided herself on her self-control.

From the sofa, Rick stared at Nola in the doorway and wondered who she'd thought he was speaking to.

He didn't have time to think that one through at the moment. His daughter's tone set off alarms in his head.

Either way, Nola was hotfooting it into the kitchen as if she couldn't get away from him fast enough and Lauren was waiting on the other end of the line.

Rick slid his hand from the phone. "Hey, kiddo."

"Daddy?"

"Yeah, Lauren? Everything okay?" he asked again, totally unsettled by the quiver in her voice.

"Sure, why do you ask?"

"You don't sound so good, kiddo."

"I'm just wondering where you are."

How strange that she would ask. She never asked, trained from the cradle to know that her military father often couldn't say where he'd gone. He hadn't even told his ex about his medical retirement from the service, only that he'd been injured, not how seriously.

"I'm in Charleston, South Carolina." There couldn't be any harm in telling her that much.

She would assume he was TDY to the base there, perhaps on his way out to another assignment. He would explain more soon.

"Oh, well, I'd like to write to you, if you don't mind. Could I have an address?"

"We have e-mail."

"Sure, but I've got some things from school and all I want to share. Please, Daddy?"

There couldn't be any harm in giving her a snail mail address. It seemed petty to hold back. He'd given his kid so little. "Sure, kiddo. I'm staying with a friend. But I don't know how long I'll be here."

"At least for a week, though, right?"

"At least a week, and I'll leave a forwarding address."

Where would he go after that? His mind actually wandered down paths of what-if he hung around here. Lauren would enjoy coming to Charleston. Teens were lured by beaches, right?

Had it been over a year since he'd seen her? What a crummy excuse for a father. He'd gone that long before because of deployments and he'd worked his ass off to make it up to her when he'd returned.

He would do the same soon when he was steadily on his two feet again and had an equally steady vision for his future. She deserved a real father.

There had to be a reason she called. Holidays? He didn't think so since he always did come through with the holiday calls. "Is there a particular reason for this conversation? Is something wrong?"

Her deep breath rattled through the airwaves, building until the words seemed to roll free from her. "Daddy, Mom's getting married again to this total dweeb. I can't stand living with them anymore. It's going to make me freaking insane if I have to listen to him call Mom 'sugar pie' one more time. Please, I want to come live with you."

Sugar pie? Lindsay had obviously found the tenderness she'd always claimed Rick lacked. He was glad for her. That part of the conversation didn't bother him—beyond reminding him what crap material he was in the relationship department.

He needed to focus on the important fact here. Lauren wanted to live with him. Now.

And just that fast, the few props he'd managed to rebuild cracked in two. He heard her request and all the pain in Lauren's voice as loud and clear as when she'd fallen off her bike at seven.

Sure he wanted to be the kind of parent his kid could count on to tend to those wounds life inflicted on a regular basis. But he knew straight up, he wasn't anywhere near ready to be the father his daughter needed.

"Happy Thanksgiving," Nola whispered softly, guessing Rick was awake, too, but keeping her voice low in case she was wrong.

"Happy Thanksgiving," Rick answered, a large shadow in the moonlit double bed across the garage apartment. He sprawled on his back, hands under his head, chest stretching his brown military T-shirt.

"Everything okay with you?" Nola asked from the sofa bed. She tucked her Laura Ashley comforter up under her chin. She might be on a pullout sofa bed, but that didn't mean she had to leave her froufrou behind, the pampering that made her feel sensually a woman.

"Yeah. Fine." The deep timbre of his voice

rumbled across the room and over her heightened senses deprived of full sight.

"Finished all your prayers?" Prodding him to keep talking might be reckless. She should cocoon herself in her covers and fake sleep until reality took over. A wise woman would. But her usual wisdom rarely came into play around this fellow.

"'Now I lay me down to sleep' and the whole bit."

More of that rumbly voice of his wrapped around her with more comfort than any luxury spread. She missed those late-night exchanges in the dark and couldn't resist continuing the conversation. "Did you used to say that with your daughter?"

"When I was around, which wasn't often."

"So make up for it now. You've got time on your hands and a full disability paycheck to cover expenses."

She sat up and hugged her knees. And yes, she couldn't deny how much more wonderful it would be to have his arms around her instead. So why was she risking putting more space between them by venturing into the dangerous terrain of giving him parenting advice when she knew it could put them at odds? But his strained relationship with his daughter seemed too important to tiptoe around.

His feet flexed and stretched rhythmically under the covers.

Why, she wondered for a moment, then realized his legs must be bothering him. He must have pushed himself pumping those weights in the dining area. He pushed himself with everything. She'd noticed all the little repairs around her house…the door that didn't squeak anymore. The faucet no longer dripping. A nail on the stairs that didn't protrude.

Every time she took a shower or did anything out of his sight, she found something else fixed in her home. The man never rested and apparently his healing body was paying the price.

He hitched another pillow under his head. "You're full of advice."

"Unwelcome advice by the sound of your voice." Her chin fell to rest on her knees.

"Sorry. I didn't mean to bite your head off."

No wonder he flexed his feet—to stretch out his calf muscles. He couldn't sleep because of the pain racked up from helping her. She'd meant to help him by freeing him from the rehab center he'd so obviously resented.

Guilt prickled over her. Maybe he'd been better off there with the more assertive care. She'd been so caught up in her car hunting and then her financial mortification—not to mention the whole stalker creepiness—she'd selfishly forgotten that Rick needed to take care of himself. "Are you feeling okay?"

He shrugged. "Pushed a little hard. No big deal. I'll be fine in the morning."

She flexed her own healthy toes under and thought of all the times she'd come home from the hospital after radiation, sick as a dog with no one to hold her after she emptied her stomach. "I'm being a bad babysitter then, if you've pushed yourself too hard. I really didn't mean for you to do so much for me."

"I'm an adult. I know my limits. You're not responsible for me."

No, she wasn't, and he wasn't responsible for her. They were two loners here together, both of them damaged and wounded, alone to heal, alone for the holidays, for some reason unable to resist taking care of each other now.

Unable to resist each other. Period.

Maybe it was the holiday sentimentality. Maybe it was logic or the memories of how amazingly they'd come together before with such compelling combustion. Regardless, time to quit fighting the inevitable.

She flung aside her comforter and swung her feet to the floor. "I'm supposed to be taking the place of your nurse. That's why they let you out of the place, because you were in my care."

Conscious of her pajamas, even if they were simply running shorts and a T-shirt with no bra, she made her way across the room and sat gingerly on the edge of his bed.

Rick went still. Overly so. "Are you sure you want to do this?"

His words carried a wealth of meaning beyond the simple massage of aching muscles. By sitting on the bed with him, she knew she would be crossing a line.

She rested her hands on the bedspread over his

feet, committing herself to the cause by pushing the boundary a little more. Even with covers between him and her, still the jolt of awareness made her shivery all over. "I want to massage your legs for you, if you'll let me. I want to be here."

In bed with him.

Rick went completely immobile under her touch. He reached out to halt her hand in place so she touched him through the covers, but couldn't venture further. "I like what you're doing a helluva lot, Nola, but we both know it would be wiser for me to climb into a Jacuzzi tub instead."

Wiser? Who cared about wisdom when it was guts she'd been lacking lately? She needed to take a chance. Gamble with life—her heart—the way that fully healthy people did.

"I have one in the main house if you would prefer." Still she didn't move away.

Neither did he, fingers gentle and warm on her skin. "I want to know what you prefer and I guess I need to hear why. No pity."

She took that as consent to continue. Talk about serious tummy flutter. Time to make the move and climb in bed with a man again after five years.

"I can assure you that pity has nothing to do with what I'm feeling right now." She sat on the edge, convenient, since her legs weren't all that steady. Just a few inches of shared mattress, but so damn intimate it thickened the blood in her veins.

He released his hold on her hand and trailed a broad fingertip up her arm. Before she knew it, her hands were moving, too. Covers still shielded him from her touch. Not that it mattered. Her hands still tingled from the heat of want. Nola squeezed, gently at first, watching his face for signs of pain, seeing none, then working with firmer pressure.

She slid her hands under the covers to his legs, finding bare skin. Warm flesh that sent prickles of awareness through her fingertips. Traveling higher, she met ridges of scar tissue that in no way detracted from the moment, only made him more human. More of a man, honed in the fiery trials of life. "I do understand your situation better than you can imagine."

Now she realized the time had come for her to tell him about her injuries…her scars, external and deeper. For so long she hadn't told people because it seemed none of their business, but perhaps she'd used that as an excuse to dodge thinking about what she'd been through.

It seemed the most natural thing in the world to say to Rick, "Before we go any further—and I believe we both know this is going further—there's something you need to know."

He eased back to look in her eyes. "Sheesh, lady, you sound so serious."

She tried to offer him a smile. And failed.

"There's no easy way to say it, so here goes." She finally told him what she hadn't told another man in bed. "I'm a breast cancer survivor."

Chapter 8

Of all the things Rick had been expecting to hear from Nola, "breast cancer survivor" wouldn't have even appeared on the list.

He had figured from her serious expression she wanted to share something big, but holy crap… Right now, he sure could use some of those psychologically sensitive and appropriate catch phrases. Because it was really important he say the right thing to this woman who'd said more right things to him than anyone in his life.

Rick rested a hand on her arm, keeping the touch simple, not certain if she wanted a full-out hug, deciding it was best to wait on that one rather than risk pushing too hard. "That's quite a conversational jump, but thank you for trusting me."

She kept massaging his legs and watching him through narrowed wary eyes. "Is that some kind of counseling talk from your rehab days?"

He offered her his best charming smile and hoped like hell his best was good enough. "I'm trying my ass off for the right reply here, lady."

"How about quit trying and just say what you're thinking." She slid her hands from beneath the covers and folded them in her lap. "I really hate it when people treat me with antiseptic correctness. I've had more than a bellyful of that."

"Now that, I can identify with. So what am I thinking?" He sat upright and took her hands in his. "I'm thinking you're an even stronger and more amazing lady than I knew."

She met his eyes dead on with a bravado that seemed a hint forced. "I'm also a lady who doesn't look the same without her clothes as the last time you saw me."

Okay, now he saw where this was leading a bit more clearly, and it also explained the mystery about differences in her figure. "You had a mastectomy."

"Yes, a mastectomy, along with reconstruction, but I'm not the same."

"Neither of us is." And that was the God's honest truth.

She avoided his eyes, her gaze skipping around and finally landing somewhere around the door—

away from him. "That weekend we met, it was my last time before…"

Holy crap. No wonder she was eyeing the door. This was a heavy-duty admission that probably had her yearning to run. Or at least considering the possibility. The weight of what she'd shared settled over him heavier than any of these overstuffed comforters she seemed to prefer.

He'd been the last man she'd made love with before her mastectomy.

Along with the weight of that responsibility came an understanding of why she'd left so abruptly with no word five years ago. She could have told him and he would have tried to be understanding, but they hadn't built any kind of relationship that would have called for him to stand by her side throughout. Yet he would have felt… Obligated? Yeah, definitely drawn at least to see her through the surgery and she would have hated that.

She'd used him…and he couldn't blame her a bit.

He scavenged deep for something sensitive to say. "I'm honored that you chose me to be with that weekend."

She stared at him, her body a sexy shadow in the moonlit room. She tugged her hands free and he wondered what her verdict would be on his attempt at sensitivity. Finally, she scooched to sit cross-legged, taking his feet into her lap and resuming her massage.

He exhaled. He must have passed her test. She

may or may not be ready for sex, but she wasn't running for the door.

He let her fingers soothe him, but his mind still hopped with thoughts about how this new information fit into the relationship they'd settled into, a relationship on the verge of changing.

Was he ready to sleep with her? Hell, yeah. But should he be having sexual thoughts when a woman just admitted something so darkly personal?

Still, she looked so right in his bed with her tousled blond curls, her long legs stretching from those shorts, legs he could already imagine wrapped around his waist.

And her whispery thin T-shirt. Yeah, he could imagine tugging that off, the trust that would come with that and them pressing skin to skin, scars and all, because, heaven knew, he brought his fair share to the party.

So yes, he wanted to sleep with her, but would take his cue from her and respect whatever she wanted. Most of all, he would pray like crazy that if she did want to sleep with him he could handle things with a sensitivity his ex-wife swore he didn't possess.

No thoughts of the past. Focus on the present. The new people he and Nola had become. And the new Nola was giving his legs the most amazing and healing massage.

How did she know exactly the right pressure to

exert? He leaned back on his hands and watched her. Those hospital techs could take lessons from her.

She slid her soft fingers higher to his knee, firm, sure. Sensual. "Well, don't get your ego too inflated by my choice. It actually had more to do with the push-ups than your looks. In my crazy messed-up mind, I wanted somebody mega healthy, as if that would make me healthier."

Was it her way of saying he was out of the running now? His ego pinched at that. Which pissed him off and made him want to push his legs to the limit, pump some weights, turn her head.

Then *turn her down.*

Whoa. Hold on. He needed to get his ego the hell out of this. He took a mental step back and looked more objectively into her eyes and yeah, he saw it, the deep defensiveness. A protective wall already erected to guard herself against possible rejection.

With an intuitiveness he never would have had five years ago, he knew. That ex-husband of hers had done one helluva number on her. And with a further insight, Rick suspected she hadn't been with anyone since. The thought seemed improbable. Five years without sex…

Rick stared into her eyes. He'd gotten better about that, trying to sense emotions rather than just the physical. He couldn't dodge the notion that he would be her first since the surgery…which hell…meant… "Is this your first time since we were together?"

She simply nodded.

Wow. Talk about pressure to perform.

Hold on. This was about her. Suddenly he didn't worry so much about his own legs and what she might think about his differences between then and now. It wasn't about then for either of them. They were both different people, physically and emotionally.

He figured the best course of action now was to stay silent and let her talk rather than risk saying something wrong. Besides, her massage felt damn good after so long without a woman's touch.

"Even after the doctor told me the results of the biopsy I still couldn't believe it was true. You know? There's this surreal feel to things, like you're stuck in a tunnel and if you hold your breath and blink you'll be back in the sunlight again."

He understood well the need to be back in the light, the sky, the feeling of freedom he'd only ever found in his job. A fulfillment in bringing someone home.

Where would he ever find that now? At thirty-six years old, he faced the rest of his life with nothing matching up. A darkness so deep, he didn't know how to claw his way out.

"I just focused on getting home so I could curl up against my husband. He would put his arms around me. And yeah, I would hold my breath and blink my eyes. Then things would be okay again."

He couldn't hold back any longer. He couldn't change the past—and he couldn't beat up the bastard who'd hurt her all those years ago—but Rick could offer her comfort now, even if it came years too late. He scooped her up from the foot of the bed and draped her over his lap, tucking her head under his chin. "You wouldn't happen to have the address of your ex-husband handy so I could deliver an ass kicking?"

She laughed, just a little and a bit tight, but a welcome sound. "I'd be lying if I said I wasn't tempted. But for the most part I'm over that. My ex wasn't a totally crass ass. He did hug me, but I could feel his distance. He wasn't okay with this. The first round of treatments, they removed the tumor and did radiation. To his credit, he stuck it out through that before filing for divorce. But when the cancer came back and the docs insisted on a mastectomy, I was a single woman on my own."

She shook her head, her tousled hair calling to his fingers as strongly as the tears he wished he could have wiped away for her then. He indulged himself and smoothed her hair, held her closer, dropped a kiss on top of her forehead.

Nola wrapped her arms around his waist. "Well, not totally on my own, because you were there TDY on a weekend that meant more to me than months of fake forced support from my ex-husband."

She glanced up. Met his gaze. Held. "Thank you."

He'd been thanked countless times by people he'd rescued in the field. Thanked in other languages. Even had a couple of kids named after him. Only now did he realize how he'd taken those two words for granted. Somehow he'd grown numb to the impact, the power, the emotional weight of those two simple words, only to have them slam into his chest now when he didn't deserve them.

"You can't give me credit for that." He'd been an arrogant cuss enjoying a weekend with a gorgeous woman. "I didn't even know."

Her hands smoothed over his face in sensual strokes. "It doesn't matter. I've learned that character is so deeply ingrained in a person…it's just something you sense or you don't." She cocked her head to the side and winked. "You've got it in spades, buddy."

He wished he had her faith in him, because he wanted to be the man she envisioned. This woman saw needs where he hadn't ever realized they existed. Too easily he could get used to being around her. Too easily he could take advantage. What did he have to offer her?

He could be there now for what her fool of a husband hadn't been there for five years ago. All right, so he would forge ahead. "Do you want to tell me more? I've spent a fair amount of time under the knife so there's not much that can surprise me."

A long breath shuddered through her so hard it gusted over him. "I think I do, uh, want to tell you, if you don't mind. But I need you to stay where you are, okay?"

Rick tucked her head against his chest, under his chin and held her tight. "Can do."

Her arms slid around his waist and held so tight it damn near broke his heart. "I had stage two cancer. It hadn't moved to the lymph nodes, which was a blessing, but the tumor was so large and aggressive I needed both radiation and chemotherapy."

Nola plucked at one of the curls teasing around her ear. "The curls are new. They came when my hair grew back."

The thought of her going through all of that alone was more than he could take. He smoothed a hand over those new curls of hers and wished he could have cupped her head when she'd lost her straighter hair and told her she was beautiful then, too.

"Rick, if we're still going to get naked together, I should probably prepare you. The doctors did reconstruction called a tram flap where they take tissue from my stomach to rebuild the breast. They also rebuilt the nipple and tattooed a simulated areola, but it doesn't look the same. There are scars that run—"

He tipped her face up to his and brushed her mouth with his. "Nola."

"Yes?"

"You're not going to scare me off."

"What makes you think I'm—" Her voice faltered. "Damn, you're too smart. Yeah, if I frighten you away then I don't have to do this thing that's scaring me."

"We don't have to do anything you don't want to, but I promise you, you could never be anything but beautiful to me. I have many flaws, but I don't make promises I can't keep."

And he would make sure he gave her everything he could. He needed to be that man for her tonight. Because all doubts aside, they were going to make love.

Rick hefted her off his lap and set her beside him. He reached over to click on the bedside lamp, the light casting a hazy, but unmistakable glow over the room. Then he swept aside the covers, his running shorts leaving his ankle on display. His scars on display. A crisscross of red, corded lines from when he'd first stepped through the soggy, rotten wood.

"So, lady, what do ya say—I'll show you mine if you'll show me yours?"

Show hers?

Nola struggled not to bolt off the bed at Rick's proposition. The words most definitely would have sent her running for the hills just yesterday. But somehow, Rick had injected just the right amount of humor blended with the reality and yes, even his own vulnerability by showing his scarred leg first.

She'd been so certain five years ago she needed health and vitality and yet he seemed no less vital now. In fact, seemed stronger somehow for having overcome so much.

And hey, wasn't that a revelation for herself?

If she believed that for him, then she deserved to take ownership of the same for herself. Strength from survival.

Her chin went up as her hands traveled to the hem of her tank top, peeling it over her head until she wore only her second tank with spaghetti straps and a built-in bra.

She'd opted for smaller breasts during the reconstruction, easier to feel for recurring lumps. That involved reduction on her unaffected breast. And yes, maybe she'd also wanted to make sure any future guy who expressed a physical interest wasn't a "breast man." Lord, she was a mess.

Just get it over with. Her trembling hands went back to the hem...

Rick's hands covered hers. "Hold on. This isn't a race."

"Okay. I understand. All right." She exhaled a mega sigh of relief. "Wait. No, I don't get it."

"We forgot something important here in the need to put the cards on the table, so to speak."

She waited, fingers twisting in the hem of her pink ribbed tank, nerves making her even edgier than the bout of lust she'd been battling all evening. "What might that be?"

"Foreplay."

"Foreplay." She shivered in anticipation—and remembrance of their last time together. The fella was good at the foreplay. Lucky her. Lucky them. "I guess it's been so long I forgot about that."

"I never forget about that."

"Oh." She grinned weakly. Trust was more diffi-cult that she'd expected.

"Yeah. Oh. Hopefully there will be some *ohs,* too."

She laughed. Laughed? She totally hadn't expected good old-fashioned giggles in the bedroom when she finally jumped back into sex again. How had Rick managed that? Another wonderful thing about this man. He had such an ease about him, no matter what life dealt.

He swept the comforter to the floor until they were left with only each other and a tangle of legs in a floral sheet. His legs stretched the length in running shorts, scars crisscrossing over around his ankles, running thick and corded up his right leg, thinner with more precision on his left knee.

All red and angry.

But that would fade with time, she reminded herself. She knew too well from experience. "You've had a rough year."

His mouth tipped in a wry smile. "You could say that."

"You're even stronger than I realized when I saw you in the bar."

"You have a way with words, lady. I'm not sure I agree, but thanks for saying so."

"I have a way with the truth." She rested her

hands on his thighs, running her thumbs down steely muscles.

He rested his hands on top of hers. "You've done enough for me tonight. Now tell me what you want."

What did she want? Total dark would be nice, to settle the nerves buzzing around like untrained newbie pilots in her stomach, but that was the coward's way out. She needed to dive in. "Who's going to be on top?"

"Is that an Abbot and Costello question?" Sliding his hands from hers, Rick lounged back against the headboard. He grinned that craggy smile that blew cobwebs out of corners with its sheer power.

"I've never met anyone besides you who brought humor into the bedroom."

Not that she had that much experience beyond him, but sex with her husband had been such a serious business. And her mind was rambling away from her again to avoid the present.

Rick unfolded his hands from behind his head and gripped her waist, hefting her up. "How about we're both on top?"

He settled her on his lap so she knelt.

"Comfy?" he asked.

"Perfect." She adjusted her legs and leaned against him, chest to chest, the core of her nestling against his erection with tantalizing friction even through their clothing.

Gripping the hem of his brown T-shirt, she inched

the worn fabric up and over his honed chest, a very familiar chest. This part of him she remembered well. She whipped the fabric over his head and flung it across the room.

Nola flattened her palms to the broad expanse of muscles. A sigh puffed from her mouth. His pecs twitched in response.

Her fingers fisted. "Okay, so now it's the *show mine* time. Right?"

He leaned forward, pressing his mouth to hers. "Shh. Remember? There's no timetable here." He nipped her mouth. "No rush." Kissed her again. "We can keep doing this." Deepened the contact, tongues touching. "For as long as you want."

His fingers tangled in her hair, he kissed her with a leisure she remembered from dating days, courting. Hmm.

"You can't really mean we could just make out all night."

"If that's what you want." His mouth continued to work over her skin while his hands explored.

"But I want more."

"So do I. I want all of you." He eased back to look at her again. "But if you're not ready, then it's not equal and I'm all about equality here."

She rested her forehead against his. "What if I said I wanted to leave my tank top on?"

His exhale swirled between them and she wondered what she would do if he gave her an ultimatum. Except she also wondered how she would feel if he seemed grateful for the out. Oh my, there went those silver chains of emotion tangling up in her stomach again.

He slipped his hands just under the hem of her tank top, stroking along her midriff. "I realize we haven't known each other long enough for you to have any reason to give me that level of trust, but I would be lying if I said I wouldn't be disappointed if you backed out on letting us come together, totally bare."

Her breath hitched, she started to talk, but he pressed his mouth to hers to silence her.

"However, I'll be more disappointed if we don't do this at all. So bottom line, I'll take you any way that I can have you."

Oh. Wow. His turning over of control to her helped in a way she hadn't expected. His understanding turned the tide for her. She nodded. "Okay, let's do this."

Slowly, oh so slowly, he tunneled his hands up the back of her shirt. She'd been prepared for him to go straight for the gusto; she relaxed a little more. The rasp of his callused fingers against her skin caught her by surprise. She sagged against his chest in a warm wash of… "Yum."

His chuckle rumbled against her chest. "I don't think my best efforts at seduction have ever been summarized in the same way as a good dinner."

"A compliment is a compliment. I like my food." She writhed against him to increase the friction of his hand against her flesh, a sweet pleasure so long missed. "This isn't a time to overanalyze."

Why think ahead? Enjoy the moment and let the rest take care of itself. She surrendered to his kiss and stroke, and yes, maybe she'd given over control but she deserved this, and doggone it, her hands were having a hell of an awesome time exploring his body, as well.

And as far as yummy meals went, her mouth enjoyed feasting on his mouth, his neck, his perspiration-dotted skin. So perhaps he'd given over to the moment, as well.

"Shirt on or off?" he asked

"Off," she said without hesitation. If she didn't do this now, she never would.

He didn't take his time or give her even a second to think—thank heavens. Her shirt sailed across the room to hook on a lamp in a heartbeat.

She knew what she looked like now. She'd stared at her altered chest in the mirror often enough.

And she so didn't want to think right now.

He gazed at her for a moment that seemed to stretch forever but probably was all of five seconds. She wondered if he would make some big ceremonial deal out of touching her scars which would make her cry and she so didn't want to cry.

He cupped her face in his hands and kissed her, bringing her chest flush with his and holy cow, he was still aroused. Relief beyond anything she ever could have imagined flooded her, followed by joy.

And desire. Sweet, wonderful, unrestrained pleasure.

She wriggled closer against him until she could feel the gentle abrasion of his chest hair against her skin. The sensation caught her by surprise. She'd been so caught up in thinking about the feelings she would lose, she hadn't thought of what she *would* enjoy. And the way he'd positioned them, she didn't feel so exposed. How ironic, how delightfully wonderful to find such surprising empathy from a guy with a call sign "Lurch."

He hadn't made this about cancer or scars, but about enjoying the moment. Perfect.

Then she stopped thinking at all.

She inhaled the scent of Rick's spicy aftershave permeating the room. No more of her potpourri taking over the room. This was a man's place now, regardless of how many floral sheets or froufrou comforters she brought into the place. The sheer masculinity of it sent a rush through her.

Rick dipped his head to trail nibbles along her ear with rambling whispers of how much he wanted her, needed her, his heated words as much an aphrodisiac as his touch skimming away her shorts and underwear.

All righty. Getting down to business. *Yes*. Her heart rate raced and her greedy hands grappled for his shorts, his hips lifting to accommodate, then— oh my—her hand wrapped around the heat of him. Something else so very familiar in this moment.

She remembered well the size and weight of him

in her hand, in her. She remembered too his growl of appreciation in her ear, the sense that she knew instinctively what to do for him just as he knew how to bring her such sweet pleasure.

"Nola…"

A groan or a question?

"Yes?"

"Condom."

"Oh." She couldn't string together more than one word at a time, either, which posed a serious problem for finding birth control anytime soon. They didn't have to worry about conceiving, but in this day and age, condoms were always wise with all the diseases out there.

Think.

"Wallet," he continued in between working serious magic on a newly discovered erogenous zone at the base of her neck. "Table."

"Ah. Right." Now she saw it resting by the lamp and thank goodness he'd thought ahead because, heaven help her, she surely hadn't.

Leaning, Nola reached, so grateful he stayed with her during the whole stretch of foreplay, never breaking the amazingly shivery contact. Her hand slapped to rest over his wallet, grappled until she fished out the thin packet.

Straightening again, she ripped open the birth control and sheathed him in a smooth sweep that sent his arm twitching around her, muscles taut.

"More?" she teased.

He slid two fingers home inside her. "More."

Much more.

He teased her again and again with a familiarity he couldn't possibly have remembered from before yet somehow he seemed to know just what she enjoyed most. When she thought she couldn't take any more without finishing here, now, he slid both hands to her back, down to cup her bottom and grip. A slight shift and lift upward brought her mouth to his again for a deeper kiss, more kissing while they continued. More intimacy. Her heart raced faster along with her breath threatening a hint of hyperventilation, because with the joining of their mouths, she adjusted her body to accept...

Yes...

His body moved into her hers again with a familiarity that washed away the awkwardness and yes, the fears, too.

A second healing pulsed through her veins, throughout her entire body, her mind, her soul. A cure beyond what could be found from any doctor or medicine.

Her fingers dug into his shoulders, gripped deeper into memorable muscles to anchor her in the moment.

"Okay?"

"Totally. You?"

He throbbed inside her.

She grinned against his mouth, tickled to her toes again that two such chatty people could be reduced to one-word responses by the power of their response to each other. Nola leaned in for another kiss, rocking her hips as he thrust up. This would be okay, fun and normal and wonderful. She could have this part of her world and body back.

More sensations tingled to life again along every inch of skin. Shivery and alive and building as they rocked in synch. Bedsprings squeaked in harmony with their movements, echoing the growing riot within her. She dipped her head to taste his skin, beads of sweat popping along his collarbone, her fingers finding the pebbled hardness of his nipples.

He throbbed inside her again, his growl rumbling against her oversensitized chest. Power trilled through, knowing that she brought him as much pleasure as he gave her.

She opened her mouth to give him another of those one-word encouragements only to find even that much speech had dried up in the fire of her response. She could only throw back her head and savor, hold, shake. Surely it was only because she'd gone so long without.

A little voice in her head told her otherwise.

But then she told that little voice to hush up. She was busy right now enjoying the most amazing, freeing sex of her life, soon to be the most awesome completion. Building now and she didn't want to risk dulling the edge from the finish. Or worse yet, lose her focus and lose the moment…

"Shh…" His voice and hands soothed over her skin as his body thrust. "I'm with you and I'm not finishing without you, like the two of us taking the leap together. Have you ever done a tandem parachute jump? It's freaking amazing."

She liked the image of their bodies locked like a joined freefall jump from an airplane. What a lovely vision of their two worlds mingling. He'd found words when she needed them, when she needed him. She believed him, trusted him.

And…oh…her body convulsed so completely around his, her arms locking him so tightly to her, she couldn't draw him any deeper as she soared into the sensation.

So amazing. Beautiful. World rocking.

She'd deluded herself once before that she could have a weekend only with this man. Collapsing against his chest, she knew this time she wouldn't be leaving him a note in the morning.

And even as she fought to catch her breath from the wonderful pleasure he'd helped her find again, she knew that untangling her mess of emotions for this complex man scared her far more than any combat mission.

Chapter 9

Breeze whipping off the marshy water and over him, Rick twisted the screwdriver on Nola's mailbox, removing the last of the hinges holding the door. He might not have the answer yet for stopping the letter-writing, car-bombing, finance-sabotaging scum. But Rick intended to make damn sure there wouldn't be any lethal surprises hidden in the U.S. mailbox, like a poisonous snake or spider, not to mention another bomb.

He'd been working his way through the list of possible dangerous surprises and general handyman fix-its. Aside from wanting to help her, it felt damn good to be out in the world again. Never again would he gripe about mowing the lawn or changing out the heater-AC filters. Nothing like a year in a rehab center to cure a man of grousing about chores around the house.

If only his body would cooperate with the length of his list. He rested his elbows on the mailbox to ease the pressure on his legs. The night of vigorous sex had tapped his reserves, too.

He grinned. Well worth every aching muscle.

So since he was done with the mailbox, why was he hanging out here rather than heading back inside with her? Giving Nola space.

She'd trusted him with a mammoth revelation, and now she was scared. He'd faced fear—in others, and hell yeah, in himself—enough times in the field to recognize it in a heartbeat. Best thing to do? Watch her and take his cue from her. Protecting her had taken on a lot more dimensions than he'd expected.

A shapely shadow stretched over him, reminding him of his primary purpose for being here—and it wasn't about being in Nola's bed, much as he enjoyed the pleasurable position.

He needed to remember how easily this woman could distract him from watching the cars driving by, sparse though the traffic might be on the back road, especially on a holiday. All the same, a large blue truck approached, slowing.

Rick knelt down to pull the hammer from the box and leaned against the mailbox as the truck neared to reveal…her neighbor, the ex-cop, Malcolm Cuvier. The truck pulled over onto the side of the road across the street, crunching downed branches.

The burly man hopped out of the truck cab. "Happy Thanksgiving."

"Same to you. What can we do for you?" Had he really just said *we* in a territorial claim staking of his woman?

Hell yeah.

"Just doing a drive-by to make sure all's well with Nola and that you aren't having any more trouble from that bastard who's been bugging her lately."

Rick assessed the older man through narrowed eyes and wondered what if… They surely wouldn't get any support on that theory from the local police since Cuvier was part of the blue wall. This would be better mentioned to someone in the OSI. "All's been quiet, other than some snafus with stolen credit cards. Child's play to straighten out."

That would rile him into action if he was the perp, hopefully anger him enough to make a careless mistake.

"Well, if there's anything I can do, just let me know." He backed toward his truck. "And tell Nola happy holidays for me."

"You bet." Rick dropped the hammer into the toolbox with a thud as the man drove away.

And speaking of Nola…

She strolled his way down the stone walk,

watching him through wary morning-after eyes. Her arms crossed over her chest reminded him of the main reason he needed to get his head out of his ass and scrounge up some "sensitive guy" stuff to reassure her.

"Morning, gorgeous." Not too original, but pretty decent in a pinch.

And totally true.

With her blond leggy beauty, she stretched those jeans and the simple green sweater out in all the right places. She continued her sashay down the stone walkway, towering oak trees casting a bower of branches and Spanish moss over her. With an extra kick of sass, she batted away the tire swing swishing in the wind. Rigged to lie flat, the tire swing swirled like a chocolate doughnut.

He certainly did plan to have a Thanksgiving feast of *her* later on.

"What are you doing out here when you should be propping up your legs?" she inquired with gentle censure. "You've already fixed everything that's broken and a number of things that weren't."

"Nothing major."

He dropped the screwdriver into the small toolbox he'd found in her garage. He hadn't found an elaborate workshop, but she had the basics. Rick mentally made a list of a couple more items he could pick up and teach her to use…for after he left? "Just tying up some loose ends to rig better security for your place."

"I spent a fortune on my security system after those letters started showing up." She threaded her fingers through her damp curls, looking left and right down the deserted road. "The cops are doing drive-bys. What else could you possibly have in mind?"

He patted the open mailbox. "A few simple techniques I learned in Terrorist Combat 101. And making use of more manpower."

"Manpower?"

"Have you gotten to know your neighbors?" If they could be called that, all a mile or so down the road in sparsely populated subdivisions.

"Um. I'm really never here and they all live pretty far away."

"I'm not pitching stones. My house is every bit as glass as yours is, lady. I figured it was worth my while to check out the locals in case you had some creepy lech with photos of you plastered to his bedroom wall."

Her eyebrows shot straight upward. "You've been checking out my neighbors' bedrooms?"

"I stopped in to say hi to a couple of the ones who lived closer when I saw them out doing yard work, wrangled my way inside for a drink of water, which led to a trip to the bathroom and enabled me to scope the house and get a feel for their personality." He shrugged. "It's not foolproof, but a quick look start."

"And you've told them my problems?"

"I wouldn't tell the divorced dentist next door jack

about you because then he might make a move." He looped his arms around her waist and buzzed her neck.

She wasn't as easily put off.

"All right." Calves cramping, he shuffled from foot to foot as unobtrusively as possible.

What he wouldn't give to have his old body back. He would fling her over his shoulder and haul her inside for all-day sex. "Not your problems exactly, because I did have to take into account that I might be wrong in my estimation. I told a couple of the older ladies who're home during the day that we've had trouble with teenage vandalism. That we'd appreciate it if they would keep an eye out and let us know if they see anything suspicious."

"Oh." She sagged back against a towering oak. "Good idea."

"Damn straight." Joining her by the tree, he dropped onto the tire swing and hauled her onto his lap instead of over his shoulder, not too bad an alternative after all.

He smothered her yelp of surprise with his mouth, lingered. Too easily he could hibernate here with her…

Rick lifted his head and his thoughts back to the crispy fall moment. "Never discount the obvious help just because it's not full guns blazing."

Hmm. Could that be a subliminal slip?

Sitting crossways on his lap, Nola rested her head against his shoulder while the swing creaked back and forth on the thick branch. "I would have thought you would be all about the firepower."

"We make use of anything we're given." He hated self-pity, but he couldn't shake thoughts of what he'd lost, memories of the man he'd been when she'd seen him five years ago, pumping push-ups on the floor.

Heaven knew he was digging deep in his arsenal when it came to impressing this woman. Maybe he needed to take some of his own advice on looking for ways to make a contribution without quite the same level of firepower. His training for pararescue might be parlayed into something less adrenaline-pumping, but maybe just as useful if only he could clear his head from the weight of frustration to figure out what in the hell that might be.

Nola wriggled on his lap to sit more securely. "Okay, you don't think any of my neighbors are stalkers. I guess that's a relief, except we're not any closer to answers."

Something he intended to do his best to change. Somebody needed to push the authorities harder, tap into some of the base intel personnel, none of which he could do until after the holiday.

Which left him with time on his hands now. "In the interest of being open and honest and sensitive, I'll own up to the fact that all this activity has my legs aching and your wriggling has another part of me aching."

She angled her face up to his, her blue eyes as clear as the sky he used to parachute through on a regular basis. "Are you angling for another massage of all your aching parts?"

"Maybe a peek at that Jacuzzi tub of yours." That should put them on a more even footing.

He eyed the marshy shore just beyond her house and wished for warmer weather. Swimming with Nola, making love in the natural watery environment would be awesome. In spite of his injuries, he could seriously hold his own in the water.

Would he still be in the area in the spring to live out those fantasies with Nola? A weighty thought, premature at that. Right now, he could focus on the Jacuzzi and a more immediate, simple surprise for her.

"I believe that could be arranged."

Fixing things around her house, getting to know her neighbors. Coming up with ways to surprise her, win her over.

This felt too much like digging in, planting roots.

Damn. He missed the old days when the stakes weren't scary as hell, when he only faced catapulting himself out of an airplane into a jungle full of live fire.

Nola plunged her body into the churning bathwaters in the Jacuzzi, her body already tingling long before the frothing jets caressed her skin.

Rick had created an amazing seductive spa setting with a Thanksgiving feast surprise she would never forget. The man certainly had a creative way with making a personal moment from things scavenged during a simple grocery store run.

Bunches of mixed flowers in large tumblers surrounded the tub interspersed with candles. The scents clung to the humidity, saturating the air and her awakening senses as the tub's motor hummed softly underneath her. And her own motor was pretty well humming by now, too.

Best of all, beside the faucet rested something that meant more than all the candles, flowers or security upgrades in the world. An ice bucket holding four...

Milk shakes.

Vanilla. Chocolate. Strawberry. And something green she really *hoped* was mint because no way would she hurt his feelings by doing anything other than tasting it with a grateful smile and *yum.*

"Happy Thanksgiving," Rick called from the doorway, one shoulder braced, his honed body on display and awesome even in jeans and T-shirt. "I wasn't sure about your favorite flavor, but I wanted to add something to the meal."

She scooped the strawberry shake from the bucket, lounged back and enjoyed the view along with a few memories from their night together that she couldn't wait to repeat. "So this is what you put in that bag of yours when you snuck off at the grocery store."

"That and the condoms."

"Ice cream and condoms. A man after my own

heart." She put the straw in her mouth and drew on the creamy shake, holding his gaze.

His eyes narrowed. "A woman who doesn't give a crap about flowers." His voice went husky as his attention stayed right on her gently sucking on the straw. "A woman after *my* heart."

She let her laughter float as freely as the bubbles rising toward her chin. How long had it been since she'd had this much fun? She never would have imagined being this lighthearted while some crazed nutcase gunned for her.

"You found my blender and everything." Leaning forward, she traded the strawberry shake for the green. "You really went to a lot of trouble. I feel guilty. All I did was order the grocery store's premade Thanksgiving meal."

"I'm sure the pilgrims would have preferred the premade, hands down, if they'd been given the option."

"Thank you." She tasted the green shake—oh, *chocolate* mint. "How about you get rid of those clothes and join me?"

"Well, since it's the doctor's orders and all."

"You want to play doctor?"

Barefoot, he shoved away from the doorjamb and lumbered toward her, shucking his shirt. "Among other things."

He popped the top button free on his jeans to reveal his washboard stomach and her mouth dried right up. She brought her drink back to her lips and his pupils widened, his brown eyes darkening to cloudy skies.

Kicking his pants and boxers aside, Rick shook his head slowly. "Lady, your mouth is pure sin."

She set her drink aside and held her arms open for him to join her. He lowered his body into the tub behind her, his thighs brushing her legs with tantalizing effect.

Nola settled back against his chest, sloshing bubbles over the side onto the rag-tie bath mat. "I did plan a more personal surprise for you later this afternoon."

"Does it involve us staying naked?" He nipped her shoulder, his arms looping around her stomach.

"No, but that certainly would make the event all the more memorable." She swallowed back a laugh at the thought of the two of them, naked, while… She couldn't even finish the thought. It would be too funny. Too much of a fantasy.

She brought the milk shake to her mouth again and sucked, the creamy drink flooding her senses—and apparently her savoring driving Rick more than a little crazy because the next thing she knew he'd snatched her glass from her.

"If we're not gonna stay naked," he said. "Take back the gift."

"Seriously now. You'll really like this." She hoped he would. God, what if she'd made a colossal error in judgment and hurt him with this? "Although since I made the reservation with my credit card which is officially frozen thanks to the creep, you'll have to pay for your own Thanksgiving gift."

"Will it bankrupt me?" He leaned back and snagged the vanilla shake for himself while his other hand disappeared under the water between her legs and…

Oh.

Her eyes fluttered closed for a second before she wrapped her hand around his so she could finish talking. "I make less than you do, pal, even with whatever your child support payments must be, so I seriously doubt this will throw you in the poorhouse. And no worries. When we untangle my finances, I fully intend to pay you back."

His hand slid from the water and he flicked the water free. "You don't have to. I owe you rent…"

"You're helping out with the protection factor, remember?"

"We'll discuss it later." He flipped his hand to link fingers with hers. "Will it freak you out if I call my ex? Something wasn't right with Lauren's call yesterday."

"That parent radar?"

"I don't know if I can claim that. I'm not around her enough to call myself perceptive. Even a moron would know she's upset."

"I'm sorry." And she was. It would be petty to mind him calling his ex, she just wished she didn't have to listen in. Jealousy made her look petty and she hated such small emotions—not to mention what it said about how tangled her feelings for Rick had become in a short time.

Okay, they were sleeping together again, not in a one-night-stand capacity.

Determined to enjoy this Thanksgiving afternoon with Rick, Nola slid deeper into the bubbles, savoring his stroking touch between her legs. Not to mention the firm press of his erection against her, reassuring her that he wanted her every bit as much as she wanted him. As if she didn't have enough to make her jittery hoping she hadn't goofed with her surprise present.

Life would be far simpler if she could just fish out her earplugs and pretend she didn't care about his phone call to his ex-wife.

Behind the wheel of the new SUV rental he'd put on his credit card when Nola's bottomed out, Rick drove while he thumbed numbers on his cell phone. Calling his ex-wife never ranked high on his list of favorites, but they had a child to bring up. They may have sucked as a couple, but they loved their kid and Lindsay was a good mom.

This new guy entering the picture, however, he didn't know jack about. Why hadn't Lindsay phoned to let him know?

Nola sat beside him in the passenger side, periodically piping up with a "turn left" or "turn right," but otherwise silent. He wondered about her surprise because he couldn't plan protection from the stalker when he didn't have a sense of where they would be. Stubborn woman refused to pony up the info. He grinned—

The cell phone stopped ringing and his wife answered. His smile faded.

"Lindsay, Rick here. I got a call from Lauren." Might as well skip the niceties and cut right to the chase. Besides, Nola had said her surprise wasn't much farther down the dusty county road. "She said you're getting remarried."

Nola went still beside him and Rick wondered for the first time if perhaps he should have had this conversation in private after all.

"Well, hello to you, too, Rick," Lindsay answered with a touch of sarcasm. "I'm doing fine. How about you?"

"What's the point of wasting time dressing this conversation up with a bunch of pretty chitchat?"

"Direct and to the point. You haven't changed a bit."

Nola had said she liked that about him. He found himself smiling and not so totally pissed off about having to play the Lindsay game right now. "How are you doing?"

"I'm fine, thank you. Very happy right now, as a matter of fact." At least she had the grace to pause. Awkward silence crackled for the next four telephone poles whizzing past. "I was going to call and tell you about the engagement."

"That would have been nice, but it's not the

point." Although it was a subpoint. He would have liked a heads-up when talking to their kid. "She's upset. Actually that's an understatement. She's really shaken up enough to say she wants to come live with me."

Lindsay snorted. "That's not going to happen."

He knew it wasn't possible, but still he bristled at Lindsay's outright refusal to even consider the possibility. Sheesh. He wasn't the Antichrist.

Wait.

Calm the hell down.

His ex wasn't a bad person, just ill equipped to handle military life, complete with a husband who hurtled out of airplanes and only spent two or three months a year at home.

Who could blame her? He never had before. Why the resentment now? He'd stopped loving her long ago.

Because for some reason he found himself wondering what a real life would be like. The kind of life she was building. Not with her, though.

Ah damn.

Nola gestured for him to turn left. He nodded, before resuming his conversation. "I'm concerned about Lauren. She didn't sound happy."

"She's at her friend's mountain cabin for the week. Maybe you remember me mentioning Becca Levy to you. Or maybe you don't," Lindsay said with one of her traditional not-so-subtle digs at his crappy parenting. "She's having a great time skiing."

Could be, and Lindsay undoubtedly knew Lauren better than he did. He'd barely spent any time with his own daughter. Although now that he thought back to her call, she'd sounded mighty upset for a girl playing ski bunny with her friend.

His mother would be ashamed of him. That burned. He was working to be a better man, a better father. Hopefully he would get there sometime soon.

Starting with being more perceptive—and he could swear his daughter was upset. But he'd learned long ago not to argue with Lindsay once she'd made up her mind.

"Okay, she's homesick. Still, I would appreciate it if you would give her a call and check in. Or better yet, you could give me the number and I'll call her. The number she used didn't come up on my cell and *her* cell is out of range."

"You want the number?"

Lindsay's shock was unmistakable.

"Yeah, what's so strange about that?"

"I tried like hell for years to get you to call her more often."

The censure bugged him more than a little. He knew he'd screwed up in being "Father of the Year" material, but he had made an effort. "I couldn't help it that there were times I didn't have telephone service. There were times I needed to go silent. Communication is better now with cell phones and e-mail."

Not that any of it mattered since he was out of the

service anyway, something he would be telling Lauren and Lindsay soon. And maybe he was getting wiser thanks to the insights of a certain pushy—hot—lady pilot.

"Sure, whatever. I'm just glad for Lauren's sake. I don't have the number handy, but I'll text message the number to you after Ben and I finish up our lunch at his partner's."

Sounded like Lindsay had the life she'd always wanted. "That would be great. Thanks." He hesitated, wishing the towering pines lining the road could offer up some help on what he should say to smooth the way with this woman he would be linked to forever through their kid. "And hey, Lindsay?"

"Yeah, Rick?"

"Congratulations. I hope this guy makes you happy."

"Thank you, Rick, he does." Her normally confident voice went tentative, soft. "He may not be an out-there, big personality like you, but life feels good now. I'm at peace."

"I'm glad for you," he said, and meant it.

He thumbed the Off button and clenched the phone for a long moment. His feelings for Lindsay had ended over eight years ago. They'd said their goodbyes. But this farewell brought a finality and—he searched for the word—a peace for him, too.

His past was finally just that, in the past.

Nodding to no one in particular, he tucked his

phone in his pocket and tossed his best grin to the fascinating woman beside him, determined to make the most of the rest of this Thanksgiving. "So, lady, what do you have in store for us today?"

"Take that right turn up there and you'll see."

He saw the turn and the sign for…a small county airport? She couldn't be planning what he thought.

A tentative smile lit her face even as he sensed a big-ass storm cloud heading toward his day. "Just because you've been retired on disability from the Air Force anymore doesn't mean we can't take to the skies."

Chapter 10

Yoke in both hands, Nola guided the plane through the late-afternoon sky with none of her usual joy since she waited for Rick's verdict on her gift. He hadn't been rude, but his brooding silence worried her.

She'd been so sure he would enjoy this as she'd made her plans. She had her private pilot's license as well as her military training, she'd asked a friend to let her use the small craft for a two-hour flight around Charleston airspace. Nothing fancy or hair-raising as they'd experienced on missions. Still, clear blue sky stretched out like a baby boy's blanket to cushion them.

She'd expected Rick to absorb the experience, soak it up after so long without. Instead, he'd gone silent since the moment they'd pulled into the airport parking lot.

Maybe she was being presumptuous in assuming she'd caused his moodiness. Perhaps his quiet had more to do with his conversation with his ex-wife than the flight.

She thought about keeping her distance…but she and Rick had slept together, for goodness' sake. She'd made a promise to herself to start embracing life again. If he didn't want to discuss it, he could say so. And if he did, then she would have done well in gently broaching the subject. "So your ex-wife is getting remarried."

"Apparently so."

Not a resounding endorsement for conversation but then didn't all those Internet info blurbs indicate that men used half as many words as women to get their point across? If so, then those two words carried a lot of weight. She would toss another open-ended question out there for him to pick up—or not—as he saw fit.

"How do you feel about that?" A simple question, but once voiced, it scared her with how much she wanted to know. Wow, these tangled feelings scared the bejesus out of her.

He shifted in this seat, leather crackling, his serious face set in hard lines. "I don't have any feelings for Lindsay if that's what you're asking."

Whoosh. She hadn't even realized she was holding her breath. "Wow, you sure don't beat around the bush."

"You're the second woman to say that to me today."

"I'm not sure I like being compared to your ex-wife."

"My apologies." His expression eased a little, closer to the Rick who romanced her with milk shakes and bubble baths. "I'm still in a mood from the conversation. Our daughter isn't happy about the marriage and for that reason I'm not okay with it."

"I can understand that." She churned the info around in her head and couldn't help but ask, "Why not have your daughter come live with you now?"

"You may not have noticed, but I'm still recovering from serious injuries."

She should shut up. *Should.* And still she couldn't stop from opening her mouth. "She's fifteen, right? Well past the diaper stage."

"Uh-huh."

Uh-oh. His conversation had seriously fallen off. She couldn't even say those were small words anymore. She'd better taper hers off now, too. "Hmm."

"You have an opinion." He traced his fingers along the copilot's yoke in front of him, one that moved in tandem with her hands guiding the controls on the pilot's yoke. "Go ahead and spit it out."

"I've already said my bit. It's not my business, anyway." There. Now she'd wised up. Hush and enjoy the flight. She gripped the yoke tighter.

"You've got that right." His jaw flexed so hard he might well crack a crown. "In case you haven't noticed, I live in a one-room garage apartment."

"Not for much longer hopefully." Wait. She wanted to call back those words. She hadn't meant them the way they sounded but backpedaling would probably only make it sound worse.

He cocked a brow. "Are you booting me out already?"

"You know better. I only mean I hope we catch the creep soon." Where would Rick go then? Where would their relationship go?

An emotionally confusing question, especially when she still had the smell of him swirling through her senses. Why did she have to make this complicated? She really had intended this day to be special, but then he'd gone all brooding and silent on her. The confined space compacted the emotions to smothering levels until she had to speak or suffocate.

"There was a time I would have given anything to have a child."

"Jesus, woman," he blurted, "you don't pull any punches, either."

"Why should I? You're a strong man."

"Thanks." Some of the anger smoothed from his angular features. "I think."

She stared and realized what was niggling at her. His hands moved in synch with hers. "You have your civilian pilot's license, don't you?"

He jolted. Not hugely, just a hint, but enough for her to notice. She thought at first he wouldn't answer. Then finally he nodded slightly. "I did, at one point.

But it's not current anymore since I haven't been able to log airtime with an instructor this past year."

"I'm an instructor. You can take the controls and it would be legal."

His hands flexed. His gaze so hungry no way could she miss how much he wanted this even if he didn't speak.

Why wouldn't he go for it? She wouldn't know if she didn't ask. "Is it that hard for you to have anything to do with the past?"

"Don't overanalyze me." His voice, a low rumble invited no argument.

Nola stared out at the late-afternoon sky and found none of the beauty she'd enjoyed just minutes before, instead seeing more of a flattened meringue look. "I'm sorry if this wasn't a good idea after all."

"Ah hell." He exhaled the curse. "Women have to make everything so complicated."

He placed his hands on the yoke in front of him, feet on the rudders and she felt control slip away from her as he took over. And lookee there, those clouds poofed right back up, all pretty again.

Grinning, she lifted her hands away, slid her feet off and the plane continued on its path without so much as a bobble. His jaw flexed.

He didn't look at all happy or peaceful. He looked more like the Biblical Jacob wrestling with his destiny.

The answers seemed so simple to her. "There's not

a doubt in my mind that you're hurting your daughter with this 'wait until I'm well' attitude of yours."

"Back off, Nola," he barked without looking away from the horizon. "She's my daughter. You don't even know her."

"No, I don't." She lounged back in her seat without once taking her eyes off the controls. "But I have a brain. I was a teenage girl."

"So you have a few father issues of your own?"

He was far too perceptive for his own good. This flight was supposed to have been about giving him a moment of peace and here they were jabbing at each other. Maybe the flight and the call—and making love—had left them both feeling too raw for reasonable discussion.

"Okay, yeah, I'm strong enough to own up. My father walked and ignored me in lieu of his new bachelor footloose world. I was a messy loose end from his old life. He figured it was better to let me move on with my mom and her new husband, since it was a traditional family setup. Nobody ever thought to ask me. Now they're all dead and I don't have the chance to be with any of them."

Much as she loved both her parents, she resented being shuffled around like a playing piece during her childhood. Could she help it if she felt a tug of empathy for Rick's daughter?

"Nola, I'm sorry you've lost your family—" he

offered her a nod of sympathy "—but one person can't compare their life to another's."

Fair enough. She searched her mind for other possibilities for reasons for his distance. "Is your daughter some mega athlete?"

A grin tensed his jaw. "Hardly. Throw a ball her way and she puts her hands in front of her face and screams. She's into theater and dance. She has an amazing voice. She's more of a romantic."

The pieces fell into place for her. "You want to live up to her heroic ideal of being a superhero Daddy who can save the world."

His knuckles went white on the yoke. "Did you study how to go for the jugular or is it a natural instinct?"

Contrition nipped. "I'm sorry if I hurt you. I had a bigger point to make here if you would just—"

"Thanks, but no."

Why couldn't he see the heroism of his survival? Or that daddies were heroes to their little girls simply because they existed? "I would have given anything to have the chance to be a parent."

He didn't pull his gaze from the purpling horizon, but lifted one of his hands from the yoke and rested it on hers. "I'm so damn sorry you didn't get to have your baby."

She tapped the fuel gauge even though it was working just fine. "Aren't you going to tell me how I should consider adoption?"

"It's not my place to offer advice or platitudes." And didn't that comment speak volumes about how he would prefer to be treated?

The plane's engines hummed in the stretching silence.

God, she'd been rude and he was being nice and perceptive. This really sucked because now she had to be honest when pissed off and sulking would have been so much easier.

Still, she did keep her eyes averted, thumbing moisture off every gauge. "Yes, I've considered adoption, but with my health problems I'm a poor candidate. Then there's my travel schedule. When it comes to motherhood, I believe my time has passed."

She didn't appreciate the way the old hurt came up to bite her now, harder than ever, when she'd successfully stuffed down the heart-shredding regret countless times before. Maybe Rick's daughter had gotten under her skin deeper than she'd realized if this young woman she'd never even met had the power to elicit so much heartache from the past.

His hand skimmed up to her shoulder, a steady weight, squeezing gently. Firmly.

Unexpected tears blurred the horizon. "I think I could use a platitude now."

"I don't have one to offer," he said, even as his eyes glinted with a hint of sympathy she couldn't miss. "We've both seen how unfair life can be, but I swear to you I'm going to see this stalker thing through. I won't let you down."

This flight, the sky, the sympathy in his eyes—and yes, making love—had definitely left her feeling more vulnerable than she'd expected. She'd never let her emotions gain control during flight before, a dangerous habit. Rick had a power over her no one, not even her ex, had exerted before.

This whole surprise gift had backfired on her, because now more than anything, she needed breathing space.

Steering the SUV along the dark back roads to Nola's house, Rick had to acknowledge he'd learned something unexpectedly valuable on that flight.

Nola had a way of tearing down defenses.

Once he'd woken up from surgery after the Hurricane Katrina accident, he'd planned to put his Air Force days behind him. He'd done a pretty decent job of that—until Nola strutted into the rehab center with her chocolate chip cookies and killer legs.

Now, forgetting was damn near impossible while sleeping with a hot lady pilot, not to mention living in her house with all the military gear and photography scattered throughout her cluttered home. Then she'd up and thrown his past into his face with that flight.

He could still smell the open blue sky even in the murky night. Yeah, that sounded nebulous and all woo-woo. But the clouds and open air up there filled him with a familiarity he'd missed more than he'd been willing to admit.

Would flying in a little civilian prop plane every now and again be enough for him? Or would it be like dribbling bourbon on an alcoholic's tongue? Could he turn his old life into a hobby or did he need to cut ties with everything Air Force—including Nola?

All moot points at the moment because first he had to call his daughter. As conflicted as he felt about Nola, the woman had dropped some heavy-duty guilt on his doorstep in regard to his parenting. He'd been so sure the kiddo should live with her mother.

He was such a mess himself. How could he deal with a typical teenager whose moods swung around with about as much regularity as a hurricane? The stakes were so damned high.

Rick dialed the number and waited for the pickup. Moonlight streamed through the towering trees arching over the road on one side, marshy shore on the other. God, this deserted area left too many places for someone to hide.

"Levy's house. This is Joel," a child's voice answered. "Happy Thanksgiving."

"Yes, could I speak to Lauren DeMassi, please? This is her father."

He scanned the nearly deserted road, the entrance to the nearby tiny subdivision, the ex-cop Malcolm Cuvier's house blazing with lights but no cars. Seemed he was alone for the holidays in spite of his assertion he had family flying from the West Coast. Something to file away.

Rick pulled his attention back to the phone conversation.

"Sorry, you've got the wrong number, mister. This isn't Lauren's house."

Wrong number? Dread and a dawning realization gripped his stomach as he neared Nola's home. "My daughter goes to school with Becca Levy. They're spending Thanksgiving together."

"Right. Becca's here, but Lauren didn't come home with her."

Sweat popped along his forehead. This dawning nightmare-come-true sucked for a parent.

"Hey, Joel, could you get your mother or father to come to the telephone, please?" He pressed the earpiece more securely in place while the cell phone rested in his lap. He reassured himself Becca's parents would have answers. The kid Joel was just confused. Could Lindsay and Lauren have gotten their wires so horribly crossed?

Waiting for the kid to track down a responsible adult to clear up this mess ASAP, Rick turned the steering wheel, maneuvering the car off the road and onto Nola's tree-bowered driveway. His mind rolled through a hundred possible—positive—scenarios.

Just as many horrendous possibilities played out in his imagination, as well. Damn it, why didn't that kid Joel hurry up?

Headlights swept the driveway, the sleeping lawn, the house. His instincts jolted to life because this time he *did* see someone waiting. Parked on Nola's front doorstep sat a teenager with a backpack stuffed full and a familiar face.

Lauren DeMassi stared back with a defiance betrayed by her trembling chin.

Chapter 11

Rick's daughter? Here?

Stomach as shaky as her newly rocked world, Nola watched the father and daughter ready to greet each other. Lauren resembled her dad so strongly, Nola recognized the family connection even if Rick hadn't cursed and explained the second they'd pulled up in the driveway.

Nola and Rick exchanged a look with a world of meaning. Lauren was in grave danger being here with Nola's stalker on her tail.

Rick didn't grab for his crutches. Nola wanted to chastise him for being reckless with his health but knew she needed to butt out of this father-daughter moment. No easy feat when she longed to tell him not to come down too tough on Lauren, who looked as though she was trying very hard to play it cool while she bit the side of her lip in obvious worry.

Teeth set, Rick made his way slowly across the walk toward the willowy brunette dressed in shorts that had probably been right for wherever she'd come from, but that gave her goose bumps in the South Carolina autumn night. Although something seemed off in her greeting. The patient way Lauren watched her father make his way across the patchy lawn... Ohmigod, Lauren showed no surprise at her father's pained progress. What was going on?

"Lauren." Rick held out his arms and Nola wondered if he noticed his daughter's calm reception when he had devastating injuries he'd kept from her.

"Dad." She shrugged off her backpack and hugged him back, but with little enthusiasm for a kid who'd made her way this far.

Nola watched the two and wanted to knock some sense into both their heads. She'd known things were strained, but she'd had no idea how much. Their awkward hug just about broke her heart.

She realized Rick cared about his daughter. Anyone could hear the concern in his voice. And the yearning for affection was obvious in the teenager's face as she embraced her father—when he couldn't see her.

Then they pulled apart and the blasé expression was back on the girl's face again.

He stepped back and it was all Nola could do not to shove them both inside so the man could rest the legs he pushed too hard every day. "Your mother's going to have a coronary."

She shrugged again.

"You'll need to do better than that. Why aren't you with your friend? And where have you been for the rest of the week while you were supposed to be there?"

"I've been following you around."

"What?" His so-quiet response spoke louder than any lion's roar.

Nola hung back, waiting by the SUV, delaying by searching in her purse—nothing actually—to give the father and daughter a moment's privacy.

Lauren finally fidgeted. Heck, Nola found herself fidgeting, too. She knew how tense Rick had been about his daughter. This news had to be rough.

"Gawd, Dad, it had been so long since we'd seen each other. You'd never been gone a year without at least coming home for a week. Never. So I called your squadron commander and pretended to be Mom. I found out what happened." Lauren's eyes outlined with mascara filled with tears. "You're a real jackass for not telling me, ya know?"

Ouch. Looked as if Rick had raised his daughter to be just as plainspoken as him. That could work in their favor if Lauren was strong enough to wrestle the relationship from her father that she wanted. Or, it could mean there would be a lot of hurt feelings before the two of them were done with each other.

Either way, Nola couldn't wait to duck inside the house and take refuge from this battle of wills.

"I understand that you're frustrated, but you can't talk to me that way, kiddo," he said with just the right amount of parental censure before looping his arm around her shoulder. "Honestly, I didn't want to worry you."

"That's bull." She stared him down, defiant. No question where this kid got her strength. "Anyhow, I decided if you wouldn't see me, I would see you. So I left New Hampshire and went to Texas. I even got a job as a waitress for a few days where I thought I could watch you. That gave me enough money to follow you here when you left after I'd only been in town a couple of days."

Fear sloshed over Nola like a tidal wave as she imagined all the things that could have happened to this child during the week she'd spent on the road alone. No matter how steely Rick appeared, she could see the fears seething under the surface for him. A protectiveness she couldn't squash drew her nearer to the pair.

"Enough." He cut the air with his hand. "I understand you think you're being all grown-up, but you're damn lucky you're not dead. I love you, kid, but there's going to be some serious grounding over this stunt. Did you ever consider there might be some things going on that you know nothing about?"

She furrowed her brow. "Like what?"

"Nola." He gestured for her to close the rest of the gap between them. "Lauren, I would like for you to meet my...friend, Nola."

Friend? Nola turned the word around in her head. She could live with that description. Heaven knows she didn't expect him to announce to his daughter that they were lovers. As a matter of fact, she didn't know what they were. Friendship almost involved more intimacy and that knotted her stomach all over again at a time she really needed to get her head in the moment.

She was meeting Rick's child. This was important. Big-time.

She extended her hand. "Hi, Lauren. I'm Nola Seabrook. Your dad and I met a long time ago when we were both TDY in Texas."

The teen offered her hand but her eyes offered no welcome. "Yeah. I saw you in Texas this week, too. You're the cookie lady."

Sheesh, the kid didn't have to make the cookies sound so...lame. How did teenagers manage to reduce competent adults that way?

"Lauren," Rick said in that low parental tone of his again.

Nola shook her head and smiled. "It's fine." She shook the teen's hand. "Nice to meet you and I would be glad to make you some of those cookies while you're here. You're very welcome in my home. I know you'll want to talk to your dad, so I'm going to head inside and make up a bed for you."

Nola made tracks toward the front door, Rick's conversation with his daughter drifting on the marshy breeze.

"Lauren, you should have called. I'm here helping Nola because she's got a stalker threatening her life. Now my attention will be cut in half watching over the two of you."

Her shoulders slumped. "Of course. You want me to go."

He sighed and slung his arm around her shoulders again, obviously trying his best in a situation that had no doubt thrown him for a loop. "I don't *want* you to go. You have to leave for your own protection."

Her head spinning with images of Rick with his daughter, Nola trudged up the steps into her house. He'd handled the situation as well as any parent could when faced with a surly teenage runaway—a child so obviously hungry for love.

Nola snagged extra sheets from the linen closet. The sleeping arrangements would definitely change since they all couldn't sleep in the garage. She imagined what Rick would want in the way of security. He would insist on sleeping in her living room after all, and Lauren would sleep on a roll away in her office. He would undoubtedly make arrangements to send her home ASAP.

The girl's bravado hadn't come close to covering her heartbreak.

Nola clutched the sheets to her chest. She knew Rick would place a call to Lauren's mom and reserve a plane ticket for the girl. Meanwhile, the three of them would stick together like glue until Lauren had a seat on an airliner home.

No more hot tub moments. Nola had gotten her breathing space.

She should be happy. Instead she felt as if she'd screwed up and lost something.

Her phone jangled from across the room. She dropped the sheets on the sofa and rushed to snatch up the receiver in case Rick needed something more for his daughter.

"Captain Seabrook." A low, electronically distorted voice eased over the line with insidious chill. "Did you enjoy your flight today?"

"Who is this?" Nola swallowed down a bilious dread and wished she had made arrangements with the phone company to have her calls traced. There could be no doubt but that her stalker had finally made contact. Did it mean he was getting more serious that he would risk a phone call? Things certainly felt more eerie, more horridly personal.

"I wonder how you paid for that airplane with all your financial problems lately. Your new man friend, I assume. I watched you both from the field. If only I owned a shoulder-held rocket launcher..."

He continued to talk about how he'd enjoyed his view from the ground. His words looped over her like an icy noose around her body. Thank goodness her flight had been a last-minute decision. If she'd planned ahead and somehow he'd found out he could have sabotaged the plane in countless ways.

Her knees folded and she sank onto the sofa arm. She couldn't bear to think she would have caused Rick's death. As much as she craved his comfort, she also longed to tell him to leave, go anywhere far away from her, but she knew well nothing would peel him from her side now. His protector instincts were too deeply honed.

As deep as her own, because she couldn't leave his side now that he needed her help with his daughter. Hmm. What an odd thought and God, her mind was wandering when she needed to focus on what this maniac was saying.

She wished the cops had tapped her phone, or that Rick was in the room with her. Now wasn't that the ultimate in selfish? She had no idea what she expected him to do, but she hated being alone with the mechanically altered voice. It could be anyone babbling on the other end of that line. A stranger.

Or someone she knew. "So you're finally ready to talk to me rather than hiding behind letters."

"Soon we will talk face-to-face and you will remember me then. Your time is almost up."

"You say we know each other." She shivered at the

thought. Was it someone she faced on a daily basis? She wanted to scream. This person had filled her life with fear for long enough. "Be a man and show yourself now. Who are you? Other than a coward who doesn't reveal his face."

"Not a coward," he insisted with pompous indignation. "A careful strategist."

She forced herself to stay calm and think, not to let fear overtake her. She could use this chance to gain information. "What have I ever done to you to warrant you hijacking my life this way?"

"I am reasonable. You will understand when we meet face-to-face."

She wanted to shout her frustration. She'd learned nothing except that she'd met him. Although with stalkers, they could imagine a connection based on simply brushing arms in a crowd, interpreting an accidental exchanged look as having a secret code.

In essence, she'd learned nothing. "When will that be?"

"Soon. Very soon." He went silent for a few crackly moments and she thought he'd disconnected, then he continued, "You look quite lovely in that color of green, my dear. You really should choose it more often."

He disconnected.

Nola dropped the receiver as if it carried contamination. He knew what she wore. He'd seen her. He was that close. She raced across the room, toward the front door. She had to tell Rick and Lauren to get the hell into the house. This man was seriously gunning for her, and now she'd not only put Rick in danger...

But his innocent daughter—a precious teenager whose beautiful eyes mirrored her father's—was in the line of fire.

Rick had longed for the days when he had people to protect and save again, but he hadn't envisioned it quite this way. Now he had both Nola and Lauren to think about right at the time when the stalker seemed ready to make his move.

He had to keep Nola and Lauren safe as best he could. For the moment a large crowd seemed in order—and on the day after Thanksgiving, an amusement park fit the bill. As much as he hated the crutches, a full day on asphalt necessitated he use the damned things.

The hot dog stand steamed a tempting smell to his left, a definite must in the very near future. Meanwhile, he made his way alongside Nola, his eyes firmly on Lauren a few steps ahead strolling past the Tilt-A-Whirl.

Rick had thought he'd put his past behind him.

Hah.

All his honed instincts and training had come roaring back to the fore the second Nola had shown up at the garage apartment door, her face pale. Once he'd heard about the bastard's call and threat, Rick had found his rescue training resurfacing with a speed that let him know he'd been fooling himself. Injuries be damned, he couldn't deny who he was.

That Others May Live.

His only focus now was to keep Lauren and Nola out of the line of fire. The police had sworn there wasn't anything more they could do. He'd stepped up the pace and spoken with Special Agent David Reis of the Air Force's OSI. They couldn't do anything immediate, either. The police were following up on the identity theft, but it was a slow process since the stalker was obviously more skilled than a first-time hacker.

Still, that phone call changed everything for him. The look on her face after the call had rattled his foundations, something that deeply hit home. She'd battled too hard to survive her bout of cancer to be taken down by a faceless maniac. Rick refused to let that happen.

Hell. His chest pulled tight. He hadn't realized until just that moment how much her admission of nearly dying had affected him.

Breathe, damn it, breathe. He couldn't afford this kind of emotionalism, not now. He'd made a promise to Nola, and he'd made a promise to his child the day she was born.

He would keep both females safe or die trying.

They weren't staying at her place. First up, he'd told Nola to pack a suitcase and meet him in the SUV. A quick trip to the ATM machine later and he headed out. Making sure he wasn't followed, he'd found a hotel, paid cash in case the bastard was tracking his credit cards, and checked them in for the weekend until he could get Lauren on a plane back to her mother's. He'd had to pull strings and stay in a dive to get around using a credit card, but he'd made it work.

He'd considered staying on base, but he would have to use a credit card there. And the bastard had tampered with her car in the parking lot at a military hospital.

Lauren had cried her eyes out. Stomped her feet. Slammed a door—kicked the door. He'd told her to save her tantrums. She could come for Christmas and they would talk then.

She'd called him a liar since he'd missed out on so many holidays in the past and the truth in her words had just about broken his heart. Keeping her alive was more important than hurt feelings.

So, now he was sticking to overpopulated places. Such as an amusement park.

Hauling his exhausted butt through thrill ride central, Rick figured if he kept the two females in his life busy and in large crowds, the unpredictability would up the safety odds. He wanted Lauren home safe and sound with her mom, but her mother simply said Lauren would run again, which Lindsay deemed more dangerous.

Tough. He was putting Lauren on a plane and

Lindsay better sit watch over the girl 24-7 until he had Nola safe and could deal with his daughter.

Rick gritted his teeth against the frustration and the strain of walking through the park all day, even with his crutches maneuvering around tattooed in-line skaters and parents loaded down with stuffed animal prizes.

Nola toyed with the straw in her soda cup after their lunch at the park. "I guess if I mention you should sit down and rest that would fall on deaf ears."

"Pretty much."

"Your daughter isn't going to love you less if you limp a little."

"Let's not go there again, Nola." He thumped ahead with his crutches, sidestepping a spilled box of popcorn. "The weekend dad gig leaves me cramming a lot into a short time."

"I'm not a parent at all. After putting my foot in my mouth yesterday, I've vowed to mind my own business."

Now she decided on silence after the top had already been blown off his world and he could actually use some extra input?

"You mentioned wanting kids." He watched for her reaction, for her consent to continue. When a passing family caused he and Nola to pause, he skimmed a kiss over the top of her head for reassurance before continuing. "I assume you meant with your ex-husband? Or is that too personal a question?"

"I guess you and I stopped respecting each other's boundaries a long time ago." She stirred her straw through the ice, reminding him too vividly of how seductively she'd drawn on her milk shake.

"Pretty damn much. Why not go ahead and go for broke?"

"Yes, I wanted children." Her eyes lingered on a mother ahead pushing a stroller while a toddler raced alongside with a balloon. "He kept putting it off. The timing wasn't right and so on. Thank God, though. We didn't need to have kids together with the way things ended up between us." She jerked to look at him. "No offense meant to you and your ex."

"None taken. It certainly would have been easier if we could have stayed together." He gestured for his daughter to hold up while he stopped at a duck-shoot booth.

Lauren—still sulking and "torturing" him with the silent treatment—leaned against the corner, feigning disinterest. He wondered what Nola thought of his child and wished he could play home videos of his daughter giggling as she chased bubbles. Smiling as she shared flowers. She'd been such a happy, generous kid once upon a time… Now, she seemed determined to ignore Nola.

Was this how she treated Lindsay's Ben, who Lauren labeled a "dweeb"? If she behaved this way, it was no wonder they didn't get along.

Rick leaned on his elbows, took the toy gun and began popping the tin ducks.

Nola chewed her bottom lip. "There were, uh, other issues with Peter and me…"

"You don't have to explain yourself." But he hoped she would keep talking anyhow since he found himself drawn to her no matter how much he tried to keep those boundaries shored up. He focused on the worn yellow waterfowl that had seen better days and downed the next, smaller row.

"I look at your beautiful daughter and I…"

He glanced over from his toy gun. "Think 'what if.'"

She nodded, her blues eyes turning paler with the sheen of tears. She flung the drink into a nearby bin with extra force.

He only wanted to reopen a dialogue he'd probably been too quick to shut down yesterday. Somehow he'd gotten sidetracked and hurt her, the last thing he ever wanted to do. Time to detour them again.

Rick cashed in tokens for two medium-sized stuffed monkeys, one pink, one purple. He turned to the two women. "Ladies, pick your prize."

Lauren rolled her eyes. "How lame."

He noticed her eyes lingered on the purple, so he passed the pink to Nola and searched for a distraction from the awkward moment caused by his currently bratty daughter.

Dead ahead waited the perfect distraction.

Rick tossed the purple monkey to Lauren and jerked his head toward the bullet drop. "Come on."

He gathered his crutches from where they leaned against the booth.

"What?" Nola cradled her monkey like a baby.

"If I don't catapult my body out of something soon I'm going to go freaking nuts." An understatement if ever he'd heard one.

He hadn't realized how much he missed the sensation until he looked at that ride, something so damn pathetic in comparison to what he used to do on the job. And here he stood, shaking on the crutches in anticipation of climbing onto a kid's carnival attraction. Talk about a revelation. He hadn't left his past behind at all. He'd merely buried it under a mountain of determination to get through one day at a time.

Pausing on his crutches, he pivoted to his daughter, "Lauren, come on. The bullet."

"Go ahead without me." She stuffed her monkey under her armpit in a stranglehold and held out her hand in the universal "gimme money" plea. "I want a funnel cake. I'll sit on the bench and wait."

Rick considered ordering her to join them, but that would start another eye rolling, slouching, foot stomping, sighing, ad nauseam teenage response of disgust. Why had she crossed multiple states in the first place if she hated him so much? "Fine. We'll meet you back here in five minutes and I'll be watching you. Stay by the security guard."

"Of course. I'll get an extra funnel cake for you and Nola." She wiggled her fingers. *Money*.

"Thanks."

While Nola settled into the ride, he passed his crutches to Lauren for safekeeping and climbed into the seat. A teenager lowered the safety bars from overhead to lock them in place for the hydraulic lift before they were dropped. He watched Lauren sit with her funnel cake, happily chatting away with a park security guard, then turned to Nola.

Chalky pale Nola? The afternoon sun beating down on them left no room for misinterpretation.

She pulled a wobbly smile. "Have I mentioned that I hate heights?"

"Holy crap, Nola. I just assumed you would like this too. You're a pilot for crying out loud."

"I like to land with wings. Not a nylon pillowcase."

"You should have told me no. I could have ridden by myself —or not at all. I'm not a kid who would pitch a tantrum if I didn't get my treat." He looked around for a way to call this off, but the ride was already full ahead and behind them. They were seconds from launch. Still, he cupped his hands around his mouth to shout—

Nola put her hand on his arm. "I want to share this with you. Let it go."

He'd been with enough newbie jumpers to know distraction worked best, so he started talking, while periodically checking on Lauren. "I love to jump so much, sometimes I forget that others aren't as addicted to it as I am. My mother vowed I gave her a heart attack when I was only two. She found me on top of the garage, ready to jump. I leaped off fences, swing sets, slides, car tops, balconies…and that was before first grade."

"Your poor parents." Her eyes lit as brightly as her grin.

"No kidding. I broke so many bones, they knew me on a first-name basis in the emergency room." He reached surreptitiously to take her hand. "I'm sure my parents lived in fear of investigation by child services since I got hurt so often."

"Is that how you came by your call sign? Lurch— like lurching forward?"

The ride jerked as if in tandem with the word *lurch*. Her hand jerked in his. He linked their fingers tighter.

"I wish. That would be far more dignified." The capsule started its ascent upward. "On my fifth jump, I started feeling—how should I put it?—too confident. I made my way toward the open hatch, ready to roll, certain I could take the elements…and I knocked myself unconscious heading out the door."

Her shoulders jerked upward with a burst of laughter.

He nudged her foot with his as they rose higher and higher, the people below growing smaller. "Hey, at least my call sign's not 'Sewer.'"

"Ohmigod, I'm not sure I want to know the story of how he got that one."

"In his defense, the coordinates were off so it wasn't his fault he landed in the sewage plant."

She rolled her head along the rest to stare at him with serious eyes as blue as the sky he missed. "You really do miss it all."

"There's nothing like the jump." Or was there? He stared into those endless blue eyes of hers and—

The bottom fell out. The capsule fell and his stomach welcomed the fall. Nola screamed, but a happy yelp so he allowed himself to savor the moment. His head thunked back, his eyes closed and…

Swoosh. The ride slowed as it eased to a stop all too soon. And that was it? Everything was over. He told himself the letdown came from the ride being so short, not a dissatisfaction from the experience. Parachuting took longer. That was the difference.

But inside him a voice niggled that there was something…missing. Something he didn't have time to explore now because he had to haul his butt out of the seat for the next person to take his or her turn.

He followed Nola onto the landing and forced a smile he didn't feel. "How was it?"

She kept her hand linked with his. "Pretty much like the first time I saw you."

"What does that mean?" And did he really want to know right now when he was chin deep in questions about his own response to this experience?

She pivoted on her heel to face him, no smile in sight but unflinching. "My stomach jolted and I wasn't sure if it was in a good or bad way, but there was no denying the reaction."

He might have a number of questions, but on this he completely agreed. "Amen, lady."

Rick tucked a knuckle under her chin and tipped her face up as he ducked to skim his mouth over hers. Thing was, though, that he couldn't just taste. He always needed more when it came to this woman. The ride was never long enough, and he didn't mean sex.

Pulling back, he stared down into her eyes and wondered what to do with *that* revelation. Luckily, he had time to ponder it a while longer since Lauren served as one helluva chaperone. "Let's find Lauren."

He took the steps slowly, arm looped over Nola's shoulder as he made his way back to the bench. His crutches rested exactly where he'd left them…

But there was no sign of his daughter.

Chapter 12

Nola thanked God and more than a few saints that Lauren was sleeping soundly in her hotel roll-out bed, her long dark hair splashed out over the pillowcase. Rick would take one of the double beds, while Nola slept on the other.

The ten minutes spent looking for the teenager at the amusement park had been the longest in Nola's life. She and Rick had notified the park authorities, called the police. Just as the all-out search kicked into high gear, they found Lauren walking out of one of the restrooms.

The cops and park officials gave Rick and Nola indulgent looks. *Too protective, overreacting, hyper-*

vigilant. She'd heard them whispering the judgmental assessments.

They didn't know the fear of being kidnapped. She did. And she'd been an adult. She couldn't even bear the thought of that hell being lived out by a child. Rick's child.

Nola's hands trembled around her cup of instant hot cocoa from the hotel's coffeepot as she sagged into one of the chairs in the kitchenette area of the upscale dive crowded with bags since they didn't know how long they would be gone. She puffed cooling breaths into her mug while Rick adjusted the lighting, darkening the sleeping area and leaving only a small lamp on in the kitchen area.

"Are you okay?" he asked softly, dropping to sit in the chair beside her and propping his feet on the nearby mattress.

"Yeah." She nudged a second mug of hot cocoa toward him, blown away anew by how much he'd accomplished in a short time. It would be so easy to lean on a fella like this. "No. I'm still freaked out from this afternoon. I know you're the one who should have the corner on the market for that since you're her father and I've only known her a day. But ohmigod, Rick, I was so afraid I'd caused something to happen to your precious child."

He reached over to grip her shoulder, his finger slipping inside her tank top to caress her bare skin with a hint of intimacy, even if they couldn't take things further with Lauren in the room. "She's all right. You don't need to worry. I won't let anything happen to either one of you."

She should be consoling him. *His* daughter had been missing. Still, she couldn't stop the shakes and guilt over the danger she'd brought into his life. "I appreciate your presence and your dedication. But you can't know that. Bad things can happen so quickly."

"I know, babe. I know." He stroked back her hair. "Is there something else going on here?"

"While we thought Lauren had been kidnapped… it brought back some bad memories, more fallout from the job." She sipped a bracing drink from the generic black mug. "I was taken captive on a mission in South America."

"Holy hell. When?"

"Not too long after you hurt yourself, actually. We were sent to Cartina to aid in a smash and grab, to bring out someone from a drug lord's compound."

"Not your usual trash-hauling mission." He took the mug from the table and knocked back a swallow.

"Not by a long shot."

"So what went wrong?"

She couldn't miss the dual intent in his eyes, concern for her and assessment, a need to understand on a professional level what had gone wrong as if perhaps *he* could have saved her. Would she have been rescued right away if someone like Rick had been sent out? She felt the shift inside her, the tiny voice whispering, *Trust him.*

"Our squadron commander went for a walk and didn't come back. I got worried, didn't follow orders, went looking for him. Everything went to hell when a rival drug lord staged an attack. I was caught flat-footed there in the middle of a jungle war."

She downed the rest of her cocoa. "Definitely not my finest judgment moment, but you would have to know this commander. He was one of those who…well, he wasn't the warm fuzzy type. He micromanaged the hell out of us. Then all of sudden we hear he had this wife who died, except maybe she was alive after all. Suddenly he had this vulnerable chink like the rest of us."

"So you worried when he didn't come back and went searching."

"Right. And got caught in the middle of a turf war between two of the biggest badasses in Cartina."

The horror of it washed over her again.

"Which group caught you?"

"It wasn't a group, but rather the leader of one group fleeing after his compound was overrun. Luckily, he didn't know I was military. I ditched my flight suit and just kept on my running shorts and the tank top I was wearing underneath. The last thing I wanted was to be identified as military to these guys."

Nola shivered. She'd been under the knife so many times during her surgeries. She'd never imagined landing in the hands of amoral animals who cut people for pleasure. "I pretended to be an escaped captive of the other guy. I figured things would go better for me that way since I would have some value as a hostage."

"You think well on your feet." He set his mug aside and rested his elbows on his knees, leaning closer. "You're a tribute to the uniform."

"Thank you." She shoved her mug out of the way and cupped his face. "And no, I wasn't raped, in case you're wondering."

A long exhale rattled through him. "I wasn't going to ask, but thank you for letting me know. I also know, though, that there are plenty of other horrors. It must have been a hellish time."

"Ramon Chavez was a strange man." She sagged in the wingback chair. "A brute on the one hand, but with these old world values on the other. He didn't think twice about slapping me around, but he never laid a sexual hand on me. It was as if he saw me as a rebellious daughter type and he was a tyrannical father."

"A father with a gun to your head." He gripped the arms of his chair with barely contained rage.

She nodded.

"For how long?"

"Time was so weird, surreal, but basically about three days." Those days rolled through her memory again, the determination and the fear. Silence stretched now and she appreciated that Rick gave her the moment to digest those memories in this quiet room with nothing but the sound of the dripping faucet and Lauren's gentle snoring.

Eventually—she had no idea how much later—he turned his mug around and around on the table and looked at her again.

"How were you rescued?" More of that professional assessment gleamed through, but with a steely determination that he *would* have rescued her faster.

"Rescued? I got away from Chavez myself."

"Oh." He blinked hard and fast. "I apologize for underestimating you."

"I managed to stay alive long enough to find a time to overpower him and escape."

She remembered well the thrill of that fight, the need for vengeance. It wasn't a pretty feeling to realize how vulnerable she was to someone like Chavez. She'd been so close to plunging a knife between the man's ribs while he lay there unconscious.

In the end, she'd palmed the blade, hog-tied him and run for the nearest city where she knew a safe house waited. "I bided my time and kicked Chavez's butt. He died later in a tunnel collapse trying to infiltrate an airbase."

"There is justice in the world."

"I guess." The death seemed too easy for all the grief he'd caused so many. "Although I would have preferred to see him stand trial for all the havoc he wreaked on people's lives. I figure that just wasn't meant to be."

"You were denied your closure," he offered with an insight she hadn't expected.

"That's quite a perceptive comment, especially for a man."

"For a man? And that's quite a sexist remark, lady."

"I apologize." Yipes. Open mouth, insert foot. "I have to confess I haven't had much experience with men in touch with their emotions."

"All right, I'll 'fess up. They made me go through all sorts of brain-probe sessions during rehab. I'm full of cool, psychologically sensitive catch phrases."

"Don't be flip about this, please. It feels good to have you say something like that, to have someone understand, because, you're right." She could get used to having someone like Rick around. "I didn't get my closure with the jerk who held me hostage. I may have knocked him out and run away, but I wanted to kick the crap out of him for how helpless he made me feel."

It had been like a return to the hospital, at the mercy of cancer, not knowing if she would live or die, her options of fighting back limited. A totally hellish trot down memory boulevard.

Her hand fell to rest on his thigh. "We military types don't deal well with the whole helpless thing."

They shared a silent understanding, a link.

She could see that, all sensitivity aside, he wouldn't outright admit how much it bothered him. So she would say the words for him.

"It's a horrible experience losing control that way.

But in a really strange, twisted way, it was also a liberating experience because I found my strength again." She held up her hand. "No. Wait. I learned to trust my strength. I would wish that for you."

"Are you deliberately being dense or you just slow today? We're in two different situations. I'm not going to have my old life back."

"You'll build a new one."

Mr. Sensitivity was long gone. Rick looked downright pissed. "How would you have felt if someone said that to you?"

"Just because I can still fly an airplane doesn't mean I'm the same person. I lost a part of myself during that process."

"I'm sorry for your loss. I know you went through hell and you're an amazing woman to have come back. But that's you and this is me. I'm not comfortable with the preaching. So if you value our roomie status, we need to end this conversation."

"That's quite a long speech for a man."

"Then take it to heart." He shoved to his feet, his eyes already on his bed and apparently leaving her to hers. "I must really mean it."

How strange that just when she realized she didn't want her space after all, Rick decided to rebuild his walls again.

Even a year later as he lay in the comfort of his hotel bed in historic downtown Charleston, Ramon

Chavez could still taste the mud of the collapsed tunnel pummeling him. Even with the luxury of the high-class accommodations he'd sprung for, he couldn't rid himself of the suffocating stench of fear as he'd clawed his way through to daylight. Having people think he'd died proved quite beneficial, however. He could move around with stealth to gain his revenge on those who'd caused him such pain.

One person in particular topped his list, a woman who had emasculated him, stolen his honor by taking him down in a fight. Honor, his manliness, those were everything to him and until he killed Nola Seabrook, he couldn't regain his true self.

Once Rick DeMassi's daughter had arrived, Ramon thought he would have a new tool to torture them, then…poof. They'd disappeared. His frustration had grown since that Rick had lost him with his fancy driving techniques. Where were they while he cooled his heels?

Ramon clicked off the remote control and tossed it aside onto the end table. He still couldn't believe his bad luck in seeing the teenage girl from the diner in Texas show up here. What if she remembered him? If she saw him here and recalled him from before, the mention could set off alarms to Nola and her friend. Time to lie low and quit trying to follow them around.

He snorted. A convenient plan since he'd lost them anyway.

Still, he could set some additional traps in place

for the final showdown, because eventually, they would have to return home. And when they did he would be ready for Nola.

This time away had actually played right into his hands.

Ramon grabbed the other pillow and stuffed it under his head, simply for comfort, not because his body nearing sixty years old was starting to creak. He kept in prime condition with workouts in the hotel gym and swimming pool.

He wouldn't underestimate Nola as he had in South America. She was a strong woman. This time, he would weaken his opponent. He didn't know where they were now, but he did know—thanks to his skill at charming a secretary in Nola Seabrook's squadron—that her unit had planned a Thanksgiving weekend party at a local hangout, Beachcombers Bar and Grill. He only needed to poison Nola with a mild dose, just enough to slow her and dip the odds in his favor so she couldn't fight back so fiercely.

This time, he would accept nothing but total victory. And he would take down anyone who stood with her.

Chapter 13

Keeping his emotional distance from Nola proved tougher and tougher when she looked so damn hot. Rick lounged against the dock outside of Beachcombers Bar and Grill and watched her throw back her head and laugh with her flyer pals.

The Saturday-night noise swelled with the engagement party for the Squadron Commander, Carson Hunt, and his fiancée Nikki Price. Her friends made him feel welcome, but he could only take so much of this world before he needed to pull his head together.

He could take a free moment for himself, knowing his daughter was safe with Nola and all her crew dog buddies at the party. Nola had kept his daughter glued to her side regardless of where she went and musical Lauren would enjoy the band pulsing away beach tunes.

Meanwhile, the water called to his soul, moonlight stretching a silvery channel for him to swim, to slice his arms through for hours on end. The ocean, the place where he'd felt most in control since he was a teenager diving into the surf to drown out the sound of his arguing parents. His ability to swim had stayed with him, even after the accident. In rehab he'd been able to outswim his therapists. The discovery had been a bright spot during months of hell.

Memories rained down on him like the gentle mist falling from the sky. Of dropping out of a helicopter into a stormy ocean to rescue an unconscious fighter pilot who'd ejected. Icy water, waves engulfing him.

He'd lost count of how many he'd lifted free over the years.

A thud, thud, thud on the dock interrupted his thoughts. He glanced over his shoulder and saw one of Nola's crew members walking toward him, the in-flight mechanic…Rick searched for the guy's name and could only come up with his call sign. *Mako.*

Mako called, "Hope you don't mind if I join you."

More like Nola must have sent the guy to look out for him and make sure he felt included.

"Just checking out this peaceful place." It was all he

could do not to dive off the dock right now. With any luck the storm clouds overhead would open and churn up the ocean for a wilder ride. "Great spot for fishing."

"Peace is in short supply these days for us folks in uniform." The easygoing guy pulled up alongside him and leaned against the dock, drinking his beer.

"Not for me. I'm out of the field for good." When would that get easier to say?

"I'm sorry, sir."

"You don't have to call me sir anymore. These legs won't be holding me up out in the field." But in the water he could hold his own. Except his job called for more than the water.

"Whatever, *sir*."

They shared a laugh, then clanked drinks together— his soda, Mako's beer. Rick sure could have used one but couldn't afford to dull his senses so he settled for a plain Coke tonight.

"For an easygoing guy, you're surprisingly stubborn, Sergeant."

"That's what my mama says." Mako rolled his beer bottle between his hands. "You earned the sir for life. No bum leg's gonna take that away."

Rick grunted, flicking a shell from the dock railing into the murky water below. *Plop.*

"Sir, no disrespect meant, but I was in a barracks bombing over there. My best friend left behind a widow and two little girls who don't have a father to walk them down the aisle some day."

Rick stayed quiet, winging a prayer for that family. Too easily it could have been Lauren without a father. He'd worked his butt off to get back on his feet again so he could walk her down the aisle.

"I met your daughter up there. She's a great kid."

Unspoken message received. He would get to walk his daughter down the aisle. "I'm guessing your call sign was never 'Subtle.'"

"Nope. And I apologize if I'm overstepping. It's been a helluva year for all of us." Mako scratched a thin scar just beside his ear. "I've learned time is too precious to waste even valuable minutes being *subtle*." He elbowed Rick in the side. "Besides, it's not like you're in any shape to whup my ass."

"I wouldn't be so sure about that." Rick stared him down with his best whup-ass glare while ever-so-slowly bringing his glass to his mouth.

About ten seconds later Mako fidgeted. "Damn, you're good with that psychological ops crap."

"No PSYOPS about it. I may not be much on land, but I'm betting on even odds if I knock you into the water."

"Well, damn. I actually believe you."

"Smart man." Rick couldn't help but look at the scar that man carried. They all had burdens to work through. "About a lot of things."

Mako's shoulders relaxed as he went off attention mode and took a swig of his beer. "I take it to mean we're not going swimming."

"Not tonight." He clinked drinks again as the rain picked up pace. "We'd better head back inside."

Mako nodded and Rick turned his back on the open water with no little regret.

He got the message that he needed to be there for his daughter now, no more waiting for perfect legs. He would never be the perfect man, perfect father. But where did he fit into her world? Hell, where did he fit into Nola's world, for that matter? Just being here tonight made him burn for things he could never have again. The water made him think he could do more.

Except until he could figure out how to fit into her world, he needed to stick to his original thoughts going into this night. He couldn't afford to take things further with her.

And for some reason, that stabbed at him more than it had at the beginning of the evening.

Nola picked at the plate of chili-cheese fries in front of her as she sat with Lauren. The whole engagement party had been a blast—heavy finger food, live music and dancing. Noisy and fun, just the sort of squadron party they all enjoyed. She could see Lauren's foot tapping under the table even though the teen kept her standard "life sucks" expression plastered on her face.

And gauging by Rick's wandering off down the dock now that the rain muted the stars, apparently Lauren inherited her moodiness from her dad. Thank heavens for good old Mako, who'd enticed him to head back once the storm kicked up. The two were now ambling back along the pier toward the party.

Nola shifted her attention to Lauren again. "Sweetie, can I get you something else to drink?"

"No."

"Are you sure?"

"He doesn't even want me here," she blurted.

Nola struggled for the right thing to say, but she didn't have any experience with teens. And why did teens layer three spaghetti strap tops that still showed their bra straps? "How can you say that?"

Lauren simply stared at her with that same "duh" look her father got. "I show up and the first thing he does is book me a flight home."

Nola leaned forward and pointed with a French fry. "Be reasonable, kiddo. I've got a stalker gunning for me and because of me, your dad's in the crosshairs, too. He doesn't want you to get hurt. You can't fault him for that."

"He barely even hugged me." She crossed her arms over her chest.

The kid had a point there and Nola wanted to kick Rick. "Okay, his reception wasn't the warmest, but you have to admit you caught him off guard—and you scared the bejesus out of him."

"Bejesus?"

"I'm an old, out-of-style lady. What can I say? But you get my point. Think about it." Nola popped the fry into her mouth.

Lauren's arms relaxed along with her practiced expression. "You aren't even going to try and fake me out?" She actually reached for a fry, shaking her head. "Wow, you just won cool points on that alone. Okay. Yeah. My dad ignores me and it hurts."

The teen stuffed a fry oozing cheese in her mouth, then another, taking her time chewing. Nola stayed quiet, giving her time to think and gather her words rather than pushing.

Finally Lauren swallowed and reached for her fork to stab up some of the chili…or rather just stab at the pile and not lift anything. "But I'm like him. If something hurts, I just get right up in that hurt's face and stand it down. I'm not quitting. I want my dad in my life and not that lame-butt stepdad my mother has picked out for me. So here I am."

"You *are* a lot like Rick."

"Tough luck for me, huh?" Lauren dropped her fork with a clank.

"No, Lauren." Nola reached across to take her hand before the kid could wrap her arms around herself defensively again. "It's the luckiest break you ever got. You're a fighter and a winner."

"You met me, like, two days ago." She didn't hold hands back but she didn't pull away, the long-fingered hand with nails painted alternating colors of pink and green to match the teen's shirts—two of the three tank tops, anyway.

"I'm a quick people reader." She squeezed Lauren's

hand with a reassurance she hoped the girl would accept and believe. "And your father has told me a lot about you."

Her eager look just about tore Nola's heart in two. Then Lauren went all blasé teen again. "So, like, what did he say?"

She started to share the things she knew Lauren wanted to hear, things that would make the girl like her as the bearer of good news… Then she stopped. This wasn't her place. As much as she wanted to bond with Rick's daughter, it would have to be done another way. She knew the right words to say now.

"Sweetie, you and your father have spoken through intermediaries and telephones far too often, in my opinion. If you want to know what he said, you should go right to him and ask him. Not call him. Talk to him face to face. Because he doesn't use a lot of words, but those eyes of his speak darn near soliloquies."

"Soliloquies? My old man? Are you sure we're talking about the same person? Rick DeMassi, big fella. Weight lifter, military dude who thinks conversation involves 'pass the potatoes, please.'"

"That would be him. My guess would be if you looked at him when he said that, you would see those big brown eyes saying he was sorry for all the meals he missed."

And that was as much as she would reveal. Hopefully enough to nudge the girl into a real, face-to-face conversation with her father.

She'd tried her best to help them both rebuild their family. But would they have a place for her?

Rick thunked himself down in a chair beside Nola, not a hundred percent comfortable with the fact that his teenage daughter was dancing with the lieutenants. But they weren't putting hands on her. Their dancing seemed appropriate.

And they seemed very aware of his glaring.

Scowl on.

He wanted to blame his daughter's dancing for the itchy sensation along his neck, but his instincts blared something more was going on here.

They were being watched.

Not something concrete he could call the cops and report. He searched the crowd, the perimeter, the trees, and could see nothing amiss. He could only sit and go quietly nuts.

"Rick?" Nola nudged his elbow. "Hello? Are you in there?"

He forced a smile. No need worrying her about something neither of them could change. He would just keep Nola and Lauren under close watch at all times. "Just reminiscing. Here we are, back in a bar again. I wish I could take you dancing."

Her hand closed over his, her eyes so full of caring his neck crinked up. "I don't need to dance.

I have crummy rhythm and look pretty much like a gangly duck."

"Bull. I've seen you dance before, if you recall, and you're graceful and sexy as all get-out, lady."

"Thank you." She met his eyes straight on and let him see the unveiled emotion in her eyes. "I would rather sit here with you than dance, and that's the God's honest truth."

He grinned, wanting things lighthearted the way they'd been that first night. Just for now. "Must be the chili-cheese fries."

"You've found me out." She reached across the table to take his hand. "We've already said all the wrong things. What does that leave for us to say this go-round?"

She wasn't going to let him off that easy. But then that was one of the things he'd always liked about this woman, her grit.

"Hell if I know." He flipped his hand to link fingers with hers. "More of that honesty I guess."

Even under the cover of the bar porch, the mist clung to her skin, giving her a glow he wanted to taste. She shivered—from his watchful eyes or the chill, he didn't know, but he shucked his jacket and draped it over her shoulders.

She burrowed deep into the denim coat. "Well, we both are certain you won't leave me unsatisfied in bed."

Memories of making love snapped between them, along with the fact that they couldn't be together that way again as long as Lauren shared a room with them.

He squeezed her hand. "I like your bluntness."

"Thank God somebody does."

"Your ex didn't?" He wanted to find the bastard, tie him to a tree and leave him there to be afraid for a good long time. Some things were worse than punches.

"I don't want to talk about him. Even thinking about him makes me ill."

She looked pale in the moonlight.

"Fair enough." This whole ordeal with the stalker had to be wearing on her. "We should probably wrap this up and take Lauren home anyway."

Nola rubbed her thumb over his knuckles in a teasing caress. "You don't care for how the lieutenants are checking out your daughter."

She had that right.

He tried to make light. "I refuse to acknowledge it's even happening."

At least she would be back at her mother's tomorrow, which would take a huge burden of worry off his shoulders.

Nola jabbed her fork into the cheese and chili congealed on top of the leftover fries. "Have you considered letting Lauren live with you at the start of second semester? Once things have settled out here and you've got a place of your own?"

"I'm not equipped to be her father full-time," he answered with his standard response.

"You keep saying that, but what if you don't have a choice?" Nola set aside her fork. "You *are* her father and she needs you. Maybe you could settle close to her mother in...?"

"New Hampshire."

"If you lived there, it would be easier with her mother close by." She leaned on an elbow, closer to him, peering into his eyes. "Hey wait, you big fraud."

"What do you mean?" He tipped back his chair, away from her too perceptive gaze.

"You do so want her to live with you. You're just scared to death."

Scared? He didn't like the sound of that. Or the niggling sense that she might be right.

"You're scared of failing."

"Wow, it took you this long to figure that one out." The woman was too observant for her own good. Being around her would be work on his part. He wouldn't get away with jack. "You must be a flipping rocket scientist."

"No need to be an ass just because I'm right."

"I apologize." As well he should, but damn, couldn't she cut him some slack?

"Apology accepted. I know it hurts when someone hits a nerve. Rick, you've been given a second chance, not to live the life you had before, but to start a whole new one. Make it count."

She was right. So right it cut deep. He needed time to let her words shuffle around in his mind until he could come up with a plan. He wouldn't make promises to Lauren until he was certain he could keep them.

"Let's table this discussion for now." He scraped back his chair. "It's late, and Lauren's flight leaves early."

"Just let me say goodbye to the happy couple and I'll join you at the car."

He did a walk-around of the car, checking the undercarriage and beneath the hood for a bomb. Deciding all looked clear, he joined Nola waiting by her door. "We're set."

"And safe. Thank you for all you're doing for me. I'm not sure if I've said that. You've certainly gotten more than you could have known when you signed on."

He skimmed his fingers over her unbelievably soft curls. "You're more woman than anyone could have known."

He braced his hands on either side of Nola and leaned in to kiss her. The familiarity, the rightness of it all caught him square in the gut.

Was this a second chance, too? He'd been so certain he should keep his distance, but what if…

He eased back and stared at Nola's beautiful face that offered him sky-blue eyes to dive headfirst into for as long as he chose….

The sound of revving cars reminded him they stood in a public place, with people all around. Not the time for these thoughts or to carry this any further.

Rick stepped back and shouted over his shoulder. "Lauren, hurry up, kiddo, we're ready to roll outta here."

He opened Nola's door for her, closed it behind her and made his way around the hood. Just as he reached for the door handle…

Nola's scream split the night.

Chapter 14

Fiery pain lanced up her foot. Had she stepped on a needle? No. It felt too deep. Too horrible.

A knife?

But the agony felt more like fire flaming from her foot up her ankle.

"Turn on the light," she panted, even as the overhead dome already blazed.

Rick leaped across his seat. Before she could gather herself to search the floorboard, Rick's curse filled the vehicle. He grabbed her by the shirt and hauled her across the seat, out his side, shouting, "Lauren, get away from the car. Now! Scorpions."

Scorpions?

No wonder her foot hurt. She'd worn open-toed shoes out of vanity to show off her painted toenails. Her mind raced. Thank God, Lauren had worn those clunky—ugly as all get-out—boots. Had she even gotten in the car?

Were there scorpions in the dirt? But they didn't have the creatures here. Her mind fogged. From the fear or toxin, she didn't know.

Still, she forced herself to think of the others. Rick always wore boots these days, too, for the extra support. They would hopefully be fine.

By the time she finished those thoughts, the three of them were in the parking lot and Rick was barking instructions. "Check your pants. Be sure nothing crawled up inside."

Her skin fired at the mere thought.

His hands began patting her down. "You're fine, Nola. You're going to be okay. I'll get you to the hospital in minutes."

Already a crowd gathered around her and Mako rushed to the front holding out his keys for them to use, while Rick barked instructions to secure the area in case any scorpions had crawled out of the vehicle. How long did she have? She tried to remember from her instruction in survival school after pilot training, but holy crap, there had to be like a thousand different kinds and just breathing evenly took all her energy as Rick scooped her up in his arms. One fact blared through the panic.

Her stalker had struck again.

* * *

The next morning, Rick wished he could pace in the hospital's waiting area. That would work off some of his nervous energy, but his legs wouldn't cooperate. Instead he was stuck waiting in one of the uncomfortable industrial chairs that was half a size too small for him while he waited for Nola to finish her release processing after her night spent in the hospital.

At least he'd gotten Lauren on a plane home with hurried, but surprisingly comfortable goodbyes. And Lauren had seemed nearly as shaken as him by Nola's trip to the E.R.

He'd spoken to Lauren the minute she'd landed in Atlanta. Now he just needed to hear that she'd made it to New Hampshire and back into her mother's safekeeping.

The electric doors swished open, a cool burst of air from outside swirling in along with three of Nola's squadron friends he'd met at the party the night before.

The in-flight mechanic, Mako; the wiry genius junk-food-junkie pilot, Crusty; and the football-player-looking pilot, Bronco.

Rick shoved to his feet, determined to meet them on even footing.

Crusty pulled up to a stop in front of him. "How's Nola doing?"

Rick nodded toward Bronco. "His flight doc wife has cleared her to leave, but stay on bed rest. Nola's checking out now."

The three men eyed him, chests puffing like a line of overprotective brothers. Yeah, they were all posturing, but he could see the genuine concern in their eyes, and since he cared what happened to Nola, too, he couldn't fault them. Suddenly he realized one of these guys wasn't married. Sure, Mako was enlisted and that was taboo for dating, but that didn't stop plenty of people in the military.

Possessiveness pumped through him.

"I've got her from here." Rick stepped forward, pulling himself to his full height, only Bronco matching him in inches, but not a chance did the easygoing guy equal him in intensity when it came to seeing to this woman's well-being.

Mako nodded slowly. "So that's the way it is."

Rick narrowed his gaze. "I'm not answering that and I don't want any gossip about her."

Bronco grinned and clapped him on the shoulder. "Well hell, now we have to like you."

Hmm. Apparently, he'd been accepted into their brotherhood. "I'll tell her you stopped by. I'm sure it will mean a lot to her."

"We'll wait." Crusty nodded and the Three Musketeers found their seats.

Uh-huh. They were curious about him. He could see it in their eyes. He understood about squadron unity. He'd lived it and he missed it every single day.

Right now more than ever the craving for his old life razored through him.

Everyone sat around, no one speaking and Rick wasn't ponying up information until he had a handle on what they wanted from him. A TV droned in the background. A phone rang at the nurses' station. The low buzz of conversations hummed in corners of the industrial chairs.

Finally Bronco leaned forward, elbows on his knees. "What's the deal with this stalker?"

"You really should talk to David Reis at the OSI, or better yet, Nola."

"She isn't talking to us. Out of misplaced pride or sheer recklessness, I don't know, but we're worried for her."

Why wouldn't she tell them? That didn't make sense. These were obviously her friends. He sorted through the events of the night and he was certain none of them could have planted the scorpions. They'd arrived before he and Nola and they'd been a fixture at a table near Carson and Nikki all evening.

Why then would she depend on a watchdog she barely knew with a broken body over her able-bodied friends? More of the pride?

Misplaced pride. Her life could well be at stake. Sure she would probably be pissed with him if she found out, but he didn't intend to bypass help that could well keep her safe.

"The guy's ramping up his threat level. He started out with letters. Then rigged her car to blow. When she got home, she found a box of candy on her bed, opened so that only her favorites were left in the box."

Crusty's foot propped on his knee twitched in perpetual itchy motion. "Sounds like this bastard is a master at psychological torture."

"I'm not even close to finished. Next he rigged all her credit cards and bank account so she had no money. That threw me because I expected his next move to be another attempt on her life. This seemed like a step back. That made me think. Nola is very much a woman of habit. She always does things the same way. So perhaps he knew she would turn on her car by the remote control. Maybe he didn't mean to kill her then because he knew she would use the remote. He merely wanted to scare her. That made sense, because then taking her money was a step closer because she couldn't replace her vehicle."

Crusty's twitchy foot paused. "What happened after that?"

"He called, using a voice-altering device, but clearly sounded male. He made it doubly clear he's done playing and is ready to move."

Bronco cracked his knuckles. "Somehow he knew about the squadron gathering. God, it can't be one of us."

Crusty's foot picked up its nervous energy pace again. Did the guy mainline sugar? "I'll talk to Reis regardless. We've worked together on some...uh...

projects before," he finished vaguely. Apparently there was more to this guy than met the eye.

All that aside, Rick had to focus on today. A lot could happen in the twenty-four hours until Monday morning. "I want this bastard caught. I'm tired of waiting around for the cops to do nothing. And I'm tired of watching for him to make his move when Nola's at risk every second this guy remains free."

Bronco finished cracking the knuckles on his other beefy fist. "Dude, I'm with you on that. This sicko sounds like he enjoys the game a little too much."

An idea came to life in Rick's mind. His hands clenched in fists in anticipation of leveling the bastard, face-to-face.

Crusty's foot dropped off his knee. "Whoa, are you thinking what I believe you're thinking?"

"What would that be?"

"That you want to lure this bastard out and catch him on your own."

"I wouldn't kill him." Rick held up his hands in defense—even though he wanted to throttle the stalker. But he wasn't a lawless creep like the man who'd made Nola's life a living hell. "That would be illegal, after all. And I've sworn to uphold the beliefs of my country." As much as he wanted the man dead, he couldn't turn his back on his honor. But he would protect those he loved.

Loved?

Loved.

Hell yes, he loved her. He loved her grit, her humor, her tender heart, her passion. Most of all he loved the way she challenged him. She was one helluva woman. And he couldn't let another day go by without doing something to make sure this bastard left her alone.

"No, I won't kill him unless the bastard guns for Nola first." He thought of the sheer agony this criminal had put Nola through these past weeks. "But I will make his life hell before turning him over to authorities."

Crusty nodded. "Then you are thinking exactly what I imagined." He looked at pensive Mako on his left and oversize Bronco on his right. Both nodded. "Want some help?"

The camaraderie kicked right over him in a way he hadn't felt since his days as a part of a pararescue team. He'd known he missed it. He just hadn't realized how starved he was until this second.

A man didn't operate as well alone as he did in a team. He knew that, damn it. So what had he been trying to accomplish this past year in turning his back on his family? His child?

What if Nola had shown up on his doorstep twelve months ago? He would have been too much of a moron to recognize the best thing to ever walk into his life all because of his messed-up view of what made a hero.

A solid team built itself on the strengths of a cohesive group. He had something of value to offer.

He was one helluva leader and here were men asking to take on the task.

Rick extended his hand to the three men in front of him, sealing the deal one handshake at a time. "I welcome the help, but I don't want to worry Nola while she's recovering." He remembered how close Nola had come to dying, a thought that shook him in his boots. "Let me get her checked out of the hospital and settled in at the hotel again where I know she's safe. We can meet outside her room by the pool and map out some plans while she sleeps."

A cleared throat sounded from across the room. A distinctively feminine sound.

Uh-oh.

Rick didn't need to be a master detective to realize they were busted. He pivoted on his heel and sure enough, there stood Nola, pale but still totally curvaceously hot in surgical scrubs with tousled hair. Her bandaged foot reminded him again how close he'd come to losing her—permanently.

She perched a hand on her hip. "Excuse me, but Nola's already awake and very much pissed off over being excluded."

Chapter 15

Nola hobbled on her heel toward the cluster of males. She hated how her aching foot put her at a disadvantage. She wanted to stride, act confident, be in control, but doggone it, the scorpion sting *hurt*.

Her brain stumbled over the notion that Rick must feel this way all the time—at a disadvantage as he limped through life, robbed of the physical edge he'd worked so hard to achieve in his chosen profession.

"I'm very curious about these 'plans' of yours." Nola swatted Rick on the back of the shoulder. "And very curious about why you felt the need to keep this a secret from me."

What was up with their testosterone dance? These three flyboys were supposed to be on her side.

"Thanks for the big brother act, guys, but it's not needed. I'm feeling much better now." A bit of an overstatement, but at least she was on her feet again. "Rick's not here to do anything but scare off the bogeyman."

Crusty hooked an arm around her shoulders. "Doesn't he know you're quite capable of fighting bogeymen on your own?"

Rick slid his arm around her shoulders and inched her away from the man. "Yes, he does, but there's strength in numbers."

His words took her by surprise, this different style of thinking from Rick than she'd heard since they reconnected that week. Was he starting to see possibilities for himself after recovery? A way back to really living again? Something wonderful to consider.

Nola elbowed him in the side. "You're not going to ditch me in the hotel room while you 'boys' make your plans."

His three cohorts pretended a sudden interest in a televised church service on the waiting room TV.

Rick tucked her closer. "You almost died last night. If you'd been alone, you very well could have died before help arrived and transported you to the hospital."

She heard the concern in his voice and it touched her heart in places that had been cold for far too long. Except she couldn't let him take over her life. She could accept his help—all of their help—but she had to be a part of the process. "I'm a lot stronger than I look, and this is *my* life we're talking about. Maybe I don't want you putting *your* life in danger for *me* any longer."

"Too bad."

She stepped away from his protective hold. "I'm not backing down."

"Well, neither am I." Rick's smile faded.

Bronco grinned and slung an arm over Mako's and Crusty's shoulders. "Ah man, this is gonna get good. I wish they served popcorn with the show."

Nola silenced them with her best glare, then continued. "I appreciate the help, but here's how I predict this is going to shake down. Since Lauren's no longer in the picture here, now that she's on the plane to her mother's, we're going back to my place."

Rick started to step forward, paused, sighed. Put his hands on his hips and hung his head. "Damn it, you have to realize this bastard is ready to make his move. The police aren't going to offer any more protection than before."

"I realize that." And of course it scared her. Only a fool wouldn't be frightened. "But I believe this maniac will find me no matter where I go. Why prolong the torture of waiting and wondering?"

Rick put both his hands on her arms and pulled her to his chest. "To give the cops more time to figure out who this guy is. You're safer at a hotel. We're going to arm ourselves and be ready. It's all we can do."

His chest felt so good and broad and a perfect resting place after weeks of being on her own facing this fear. Her foot hurt. Her heart hurt. But she wouldn't be shoved aside.

She pushed back. "You're not cutting me out, Rick."

His jaw jutted. "You're a wounded trooper."

"Damn it, I'm wounded, not incapacitated. Don't you remember how it feels not to be able to get into the action? Don't do this to me. If we're back at my house, at least we have the familiarity of the terrain on our side and you gain the advantage of having an extra warrior. *Me.*"

She stared him down and she could see that he would agree, but only because she'd given him no choice.

"Okay," Rick said. "You can have a role—within reason. But one sign of wavering on your feet and I'm tossing your butt in bed."

Her heart throbbed even more than her wounded foot—and that was pretty damn bad. What kind of future would she have with this man if he always insisted on pushing her aside? Would he be able to open up to his daughter? And what if the day came when the adoption issue arose…

Ohmigod, she was thinking marriage and he wasn't even able to allow her anything more than a begrudging role because she'd left him no choice. Still something about this man called to her. His inner strength, a depth of character that Peter hadn't come close to possessing. It had nothing to do with muscles and everything to do with Rick's great big heart. He simply couldn't hide behind that gruff exterior.

None of which she could afford to think about now. They had plans to make, her lover and her friends who were putting their lives on the line for her. They needed to come up with a strategy to trap her stalker before he could make his move. And after they made their plan?

They would wait.

Rick had been prepared for the bastard to strike fast, but he hadn't expected the guy would make his move on the first night Nola got out of the hospital. Her home phone rang with an "unknown number." His gut told him right away it wasn't a telemarketer.

Their guy was on the move.

He nodded for her to pick up while he made quick calls on the cell phone to their buddies out in the woods to alert them.

"Hello," Nola answered, then shook her head at him to signify…it wasn't their guy after all? Damn. "Yes, this is Nola Seabrook. Rick's right here."

She passed him the phone and before it even reached his ear he could hear Lindsay's hysterical voice sobbing on the other end. Holy crap. He forced the knot in his throat down with a heavy swallow.

"Lindsay, what's wrong?"

"Lauren," she gasped between sobs, "didn't get off

the plane. They said she never got on in Atlanta. That means she's been missing for over six hours with the layover, Rick. Oh my God, where is our baby?"

The bottom dropped out of his gut, his whole world sinking, sliding out from under him faster than the ground had given way beneath his feet the day his legs had gone to hell.

He knew. Nola's stalker had made his move after all. He had outthought them in a way they should have foreseen. Rick never should have let Lauren fly alone. Damn it. Why hadn't the attendants stayed with her as they were supposed to? He'd paid the extra fee to have her watched over and hand escorted to her next flight.

All a moot point now.

"We'll find her," he insisted to Lindsay, even as he feared all sorts of nightmares.

Nola's eyes met his while he continued to talk, her hand closing over his with comfort.

"She could be anywhere." Lindsay's thoughts echoed his own, the first time they'd agreed on anything in years.

"I realize that. But is there anything else you can tell me?"

"No," she wailed. "The police are investigating. The cops here will be contacting the authorities there and I didn't want you to be surprised by that visit."

"Thank you." And please, Lord, they still wouldn't have a visit from cops with far worse news. He refused to accept that could happen.

Nola swayed on her feet. Rick reached for her but she collapsed into a chair. Already he could see the guilt building to irrational proportions in her eyes.

"Lindsay, is Ben with you?"

"Of course."

"Okay. Hang tough and I'll let you know if we hear anything."

"Us, too."

They disconnected. He met Nola's gaze and held, injecting as much steadiness as he could under the circumstances. "It's not your fault."

"We don't have time to waste discussing this. Let's get the search moving."

Odd how she knew as well as he did Lauren wouldn't be in Atlanta long. The bastard who had been stalking Nola would bring Lauren back here to taunt them.

He reached for his cell phone again to recall Bronco, Crusty and Mako from their posts in the woods and up the road.

Within seconds they were in Nola's living room, too, pacing, while Rick hung up from calling the police. He dropped into a chair, his brain racing.

Crusty plowed his hand through his mess of hair. "I'll head over to check in with the OSI. We've already got things rolling with David Reis so here's a good place to start. He got a lead on the Internet crimes and traced the server to a local hotel. We'll see if there's more to follow up on that."

Bronco's eyes lit with a parental concern, obviously a father himself. "Mako and I will make an end run to the airport. It's a long shot that we can catch him there, but you never know."

Rick clenched his cell phone. "We'll stay here and wait for the police. I don't want to leave in case she shows up here again. Let's hope she's just run off."

As her squadron comrades drove out onto the street, Nola slid her arm around Rick's waist in comfort. She sat on the arm of the chair beside him. "I am so sorry. I can only imagine what kind of hell you're going through right now."

Hell didn't even come close to describing this. Hoping at best Lauren was alone on the run. Fearing at the worst she was in the hands of a maniac who blew up cars and planted scorpions. He lost track of how long they sat there letting everything sink in, but they both needed a moment to gather their thoughts before…doing what?

"Rick! The window." She nudged him. "Your gun. Get your gun."

He looked up from the rug and saw…hell come to life in front of his eyes. An older man stood in the middle of her front yard, framed by the curtains—

Holding a gun to Lauren's head.

Chapter 16

Nola blinked, hard. And still the unbelievable nightmare stayed in front of her eyes.

The man outside the window was supposed to be long dead, smothered in a collapsed tunnel in South America. But her vision didn't lie. Ramon Chavez, the drug lord who'd taken her hostage a year ago, had somehow survived and now had a gun to Lauren's head.

The teen appeared dazed, as if she'd been drugged with a mild sedative. Apparently the bastard wasn't underestimating women this time. Suddenly the scorpion sting made sense, too. He'd taken time to import the deadly critters from his part of the world, a message she hadn't understood, damn it.

Guilt sliced deeper than any poisonous sting. How could she have brought this hell to Rick's daughter? Every tear streak down the girl's face made Nola's heart squeeze tighter. And a coat. The child needed a coat to cover her in those little tank tops she favored.

What a silly thought as the teen shivered in fear with a gun pressed to her head, but the maternal instinct flowered to life so fiercely, it was all Nola could do to keep from launching across the lawn to rip out Chavez's throat.

Nola couldn't imagine why in hell the man would come here for her, but then he hadn't been sane in those days she'd spent with him before. Time for musing would come later. Only Lauren counted now.

"Rick," she whispered under her breath, trying not to move her mouth in case it upset the man outside. Slowly, she moved toward the door with him. "His name is Ramon Chavez. It's the South American drug lord who held me captive a year ago. We all thought he died. He's wily and he's strong. Don't underestimate him because of his age."

"Got it." Rick tucked his weapon out of sight in the small of his back. "We can't go out with it showing. He'll only make me throw it down."

Somewhere in his fifties, the man looked as if he stayed in shape. She'd fought hard to escape Ramon Chavez, a narrow thing a year ago when she'd been in top condition, and now she could barely walk after the scorpion sting. Rick had an amazing amount of upper body strength, but one swipe to his legs…

She couldn't afford these negative thoughts.

Her hand closed over the doorknob.

Rick's hand rested on her waist. "Stay on the other side of me, away from him. I can't worry about you and Lauren. I love you."

He opened the door.

Good God. He dropped the "love bomb" like that and expected her to keep her cool? Nola scrambled for her scattered wits and—what do you know?—Rick used her hesitation to put himself between her and the gunman.

Rick braced a hand on the porch post.

Nola pulled up alongside him. "So you've finally decided to show your face."

"I decided the time had come." He caressed the gun along Lauren's forehead in a sadistic show of force. "My timing. My control. You may have gotten the better of me once, but I *will* be the victor this time."

Nola sifted through his words and could hardly believe how the pieces fit together. The man had come after her because of a wounded ego?

She stepped onto the porch, staying behind Rick, not because she felt she needed his shielding but because she didn't want him distracted with worry. "How did you survive the tunnel collapse?"

"I am a strong man, stronger than anyone gave me

credit for." He hitched his arm harder against the terrified teen's gut. "I clawed my way to freedom. Revenge can give you more strength than you could imagine."

She hoped he was right because the need for a slice of vengeance for herself gnawed deep.

At the show of force against Lauren, a vein popped along Rick's temple. "How did you get to my daughter?"

Chavez tut-tutted. "You two are so predictable. I knew you would send the child away. I am an Internet genius. When you booked her flight, I booked my own on her flight. It was no problem to overtake her in Atlanta when she went to the restroom on her own. I simply waylaid Lauren and told her that her father had been in an accident. Your daughter is truly too trusting."

Nola rested her hand on Rick's back in reassurance.

"I do not want to hurt this pretty young child. She has done nothing to me, but you know as well as I that there are casualties in war. It is up to you as to whether she will be one of them. Will you come quietly with me now? Or will you make this a fight?"

Their first order of business had to be securing the safety of Rick's daughter. Nola knew that. She had beaten this man once before, she could do it again. She refused to think about what the scorpion's poison had done to her system. Of course that would have been the man's plan, to weaken her this time. Now it all made sense.

She came level, shoulder to shoulder with Rick, then moved down to the first step.

"I love you, too," she whispered as she passed, and ohmigod what a time to make this realization.

They should have had more time... She had to think positively. Put one foot in front of the other.

Chavez eased his hold on the girl. Nola wondered if she could trust his word. What if he took them both hostage? But this man had always entertained a twisted sense of frontier justice. Somehow she believed he would let Lauren go. He meant what he said about his vendetta being with her alone. His reasons for killing her were bizarre to say the least, but his obsession was with her alone.

She also knew Rick's code of honor was unbending. He would not leave with her still held hostage. He would die first. Without question.

Her feet faltered. How could she guarantee both the father's and daughter's safety? She couldn't.

Her heart squeezed.

Lauren walked past her, tears streaking mascara down the young girl's no-longer-jaded-face. Their hands brushed. Then Lauren ran for her father.

Nola closed the last few steps between herself and the man who'd held her hostage a year ago. Helplessness threatened to swallow her. Her worst fears came to life again. Battling free of him before had been so liberating. Why did she have to go through this again?

She couldn't let the negativity show through or it would distract Rick.

Chavez gripped her upper arm, his fingers a steely, unforgiving band. "You won't get away this time." He jabbed the gun deeper into her waist. "Major DeMassi, I'm sure you have a gun tucked somewhere. Toss it aside. Now please, or I will start shooting."

Nola watched Rick calculating until finally, he reached behind him and took the weapon from the small of his back and placed it on the porch banister, carefully. She made note of it, hoping one of them could use it later.

Soon, hopefully. She shivered against the stench of Chavez's breath and the sheer evil and hatred radiating from him. She wanted to fight him again. She assessed the strength of his hold on her. He obviously still worked out. He'd been strong before—and seemed more so now. Getting away from him before had been a near thing with her at full speed. She had to be honest with herself. The scorpion sting had drained her. Even now, lethargy stole over her.

Could Rick hold his own against the man? Would his legs support him? She saw the determination in his eyes as he wordlessly shoved Lauren behind him. She saw the implicit instruction there. He had a plan. He wanted her to see to Lauren and he would take care of Chavez.

Then it hit her. Rick trusted her with his child. Something fluttered to life inside her that she hadn't even realized was dead. Her ex-husband had refused so many times to have children with her, only to start a family right away with his new wife. That had hurt in a way she'd never fully acknowledged. And now Rick trusted her with his child.

A small moment. A big step. One she would savor later, because yes, she intended to have a later with this man and his child, and her own second chance at life.

Nola looked him in the eyes and let him read her implicit message, her joining in his plan. The communication flowed freely between them in a way she'd never felt with her ex-husband. She hadn't even known what she was missing.

Chavez yanked her arm. "We're going to leave now. I am a man of honor and I meant what I said about only wanting Nola." He nodded to Rick. "However, if I were you, I wouldn't try starting that car of yours anytime soon."

Time to put this plan into action. She let her eyelids grow heavy, her body sag ever so increasingly in Chavez's grip.

"Stop that!" he ordered.

"What? Huh?" She shook herself a little as if trying to shore herself up, then drooped again.

"Damn it, woman."

Rick frowned, taking a step forward. "It must be

the scorpion bite you inflicted on her. You wanted her weakened. You did this to her."

"No closer," Chavez warned. "She and I are going to leave now."

Like hell.

Her eyes snapped open and made direct contact with Rick's.

Now! her unspoken message shouted.

Rick shoved Lauren to the right as Nola chopped Chavez's gun hand down. The gunshot split the air, sending rock and dirt flying as Rick launched forward. Chavez's weapon skittered away and into the water.

Nola dropped and rolled out of the way, toward Lauren. She covered the child's body with hers. Watching. Praying.

Rick and Chavez exchanged punches and ohmigod, the older man seemed to be gaining ground. Blood poured from a cut above Rick's eye. Another punch landed in his gut. Grunting, Rick stumbled backward a good five steps...

Backward?

Toward the watery drop-off.

Realization dawned. Rick wasn't losing the fight at all. He was taking it to his playing field where he knew he stood better odds of winning. Two more punches put Rick's heels on the edge of the water while Lauren screamed in fear as she tried to run for her father. Nola pinned the hysterical teen to the ground even as she, too, longed to run and offer help.

In a flash, his fist shot out and gripped Chavez's shirt and they both went over backward. The splash swallowed both men, the water deep from the recent swell of rain.

She held her breath as if in sympathy. The murky waters churned with action. Bubbles roiled with no signs of a victor or loser. What if she was wrong and Rick couldn't pull this off? His injuries had been extensive. How long could they stay under? How long had passed? The cooler temperatures would play havoc with their bodies.

Lauren whimpered under her.

Nola sat up and hugged her close. "It's okay, sweetie, your daddy's an expert at this. He's trained for these kinds of waters. This is exactly where he wanted the fight to be."

"He's a hero."

"Absolutely."

A hero. But also a man who had entrusted his child to her. Keeping a hand firmly locked around Lauren's wrist, Nola jerked her up to run to the porch and retrieve Rick's gun, because as much as she prayed that he would come out of those waters alive, she knew that life wasn't fair and predictable. She'd made him a promise to keep his daughter safe.

Nola pulled her cell phone from her pocket and

passed it to Lauren. "Call the police again and update them."

Then she wrapped an arm around the teen's shoulder and gripped the gun in her other hand. Waiting for the man she loved. The power of it didn't come over her in some gentle breeze or pretty flowering. It smashed her over the head then squeezed tight, a strong emotion as big and powerful as the man who'd brought it.

In a gush upward, Rick exploded from the water, alive. Thank God, alive.

Vital.

Hers.

Emotions swirled inside her, bubbling higher and higher until tears flowed down her face and the gun shook in her hand. His angular features wet, his hair streaming and jet-black. In his fist, he held the limp body of her captor.

"Unconscious, not dead," Rick gasped, then grinned. "God, you look hot holding that gun, all fired up and protecting my kid. Wanna get hitched?"

Choking back the tears of relief, Nola launched forward with Lauren while Rick tossed the unconscious Chavez onto the bank. Rick took the gun from her shaking hand and trained it on the bastard sprawled on the sandy shore, gathering up Nola and Lauren with his other arm.

Nola let the tears of relief flow and hugged Rick back, Lauren, too, this unexpected child who had come into her life. A stepdaughter. Wow. Mind-blowing. Exciting.

Sirens whined in the distance, but Nola barely noticed with her cheek pressed to Rick's wet chest, his heart thudding in her ear. A heart she would listen to for the rest of her life.

Leaning against a tree by the marsh, Rick wondered at the hitch in his throat that lingered long after the cops had cleared out with Chavez in hand-cuffs. Lauren and Nola were inside cleaning up.

He'd already called Lindsay and told her he would send Lauren home tomorrow. His ex-wife had gone a little hysterical after hearing what happened, but her husband-to-be had taken the phone and offered an awkward thank-you. Something that meant a lot coming from the guy who would be spending so much time with Lauren over the next few years.

Rick figured he would use the time-out near the water to gather his thoughts. The water had served him well in the end, always his friend. Always home.

Except that wasn't quite true anymore. He'd found a new home.

With Nola.

"Dad?"

He pivoted to find Lauren waiting at the bottom porch step, her long hair wet from her shower. She wore her standard sleep pants and a raggedy T-shirt...

Wait. Wasn't that…? It was. An old T-shirt of his from an air show they'd attended together.

And she still wore it.

He had two choices right now. He could stand here and feel guilty. Or he could move forward on his battered legs and fix things with his daughter.

Rick took a step, not bothering to grab for a tree to hide the limp. He just let it show, the reality of his injuries, and walked to his daughter. He also looked into her eyes with the new way of seeing that he'd learned from Nola and saw…

The same hero worship he'd found when he'd swept her up at five years old. It had been there all along.

He held open his arms.

Lauren ran into them without hesitation and sobbed against his chest. "I'm sorry, Daddy, I'm so sorry."

"I know, kiddo, I know."

"I didn't mean to make things worse here, I just wanted to see you, I just…" She babbled on and on and he let her, stroking her hair the way he had when she was little and scraped her knee.

The instincts to parent were there. He'd just been too scared to listen because messing this up came with stakes higher than any out in the field.

Finally, her tears slowed, but he sensed the need to talk more. Inspiration struck. "How about we step over here."

He gestured to the tire swing. Her eyebrows knit together, but she shuffled over to sit. Rick planted a hand between her shoulder blades and gave a gentle shove to launch her just as he'd done hundreds of times when she'd been a toddler.

"I've been thinking, kiddo."

She swished back, her face wary. "And?"

"Good thoughts. No worries." He gave the swing another nudge, higher. He remembered she enjoyed higher, like him. The rope creaked on the branch. "How about you come see me for Christmas break? Two full weeks of no pressure, no stalkers and we see how it goes. If everything works out, we can talk to your mother about your staying with me for a semester."

She swung back toward him. Her feet dragging to slow the momentum. "Do you mean it? Really?"

He grabbed the rope to bring the swing to a complete stop. "I may not have always been there for you, but I kept my promises when I made them."

She rested her head on the rope and grinned. "Cool."

A resounding endorsement from a teen. He didn't delude himself that it would be all smooth sailing, but he was learning. Lauren was trying.

He was scared as hell—and so damn excited to have more time with his child.

She leaped from the swing and gave him a quick, almost bashful kiss on his cheek so quickly he nearly missed it.

"Night, Daddy."

Lauren bolted across the yard and up the steps and

into the house. Rick dropped into the swing, the tire laying flat, tied in three places.

Damn. This parenting gig was more exhausting than battling a South American drug lord.

And the strangest thing of all, he wanted to share this moment with Nola. He needed to hear her feedback on what he'd said to his daughter. How amazing that the woman could have become such an integral part of his life in such a short time.

Still he could hear the words they'd exchanged in the heat of battle.

I love you.

He'd meant it.

Then there she was, framed in her doorway with her hair damp, curls clinging to her face in swirls. Lord, she did things to jeans with those long legs of hers that should be illegal out in public.

"Wanna hitch a ride, lady?" He patted his lap.

"That ride looks far better than that bullet thing you lured me into trying."

Grinning, she hobbled across the porch, one foot bandaged from the sting and in a flip-flop. She limped across the sparse lawn, her foot apparently still throbbing from the scorpion sting. Residual anger stirred in him that wouldn't go away anytime soon, probably not until the trial ended with Chavez locked up for life. But Rick refused to let it spoil his plans for tonight.

She settled across his lap, looping her arms around

his neck. Her head fell to rest on his shoulders. "Hmm... Yes, this ride I like. How bizarre to feel so content and exhausted at the same time."

"I hear you." He rested his chin on her head, the sweet smell of flowery shampoo teasing his nose. He scuffed his boot against the dusty ground and set the swing into motion.

"You were something, the way you brought him down in the water." She wrapped her arms around his waist.

"I figured the water was my best bet at leveling the playing field."

"I know. I saw that in your eyes."

He'd thought they communicated there in that moment, but he hadn't been sure. Now he knew she felt the same connection. They had something special and he intended to hold it fast.

She hugged his waist tighter and pressed a kiss to his neck, snuggling closer. They stayed linked like that for...he wasn't sure how long but the familiarity felt so good he went with it until the moment seemed right to continue.

"I like your place here."

"You do?" She smiled against his neck. "Are you angling to take up a permanent residence?"

He'd already asked her to tie the knot in the adrenaline surge after knocking out Chavez, but he understood this practical woman needed details. Grounding. And maybe because she was a warrior, too, she understood the primal desire to stake a claim on life after a battle with death. Maybe she didn't know if she could trust his off-the-cuff proposal.

She would find out soon enough.

"I'm not much for being a kept man. I've been doing a lot of thinking out here tonight. It's amazing how fast plans can come together when you think you might lose everything that counts."

His arms convulsed around her, though he tried not to hold her too tightly. It was tough when his brain kept replaying the horror of seeing a gun pressed to her head, to his daughter's head. His whole world had almost been blown away tonight.

He forced himself to relax and continue. He wouldn't let this second chance slip away. "I've got a plan for my future. Or at least the start of one. I'm in a unique position. With my disability pay, I don't need to make big bucks. I can pick any profession. I want to train volunteer search-and-rescue teams out of that small airport where we flew on Thanksgiving. I'll even be able to do some jumps on occasion once my body finishes healing."

"Where does that leave us with moving in together?"

Her fingers traced over his heart, shaking ever so slightly. He clasped her hand and brought it to his mouth for a kiss, linking their fingers before continuing.

"I would have to contribute something to the equation. I spent so much time on the road, I never spent much on myself. I've got some money saved up." He gestured out to the water's edge. "Maybe I could put in a dock there." Then over to the large stretch of patchy lawn where grass never seemed to grow well. "Perhaps a pool here."

"Lauren would like that," she said with unmistakable nudging.

"Yeah, she would." And here things got complicated. "What would you think if she came to live here for a trial semester?"

"I would think that would be great for her."

"What about for you?" He wanted her to be a part of his life and still she hadn't mentioned his impromptu proposal when he'd hauled himself out of the water.

"That girl has a way of working her way into a person's heart very quickly." Nola eased back to look up into his face with what he hoped was love in her eyes. "Very much like her father."

Time to take a leap bigger than any he'd ever attempted, and he'd managed some mighty death-defying jumps in his time. "I meant what I said there at the end. That wasn't adrenaline talking."

Her gaze skated out to the murky waters. "It surely made for a memorable proposal."

He mentally thumped himself as he realized perhaps he should have given this more thought. "Would you like something more romantic?"

She shook her head, her damp curls beginning to

dry and rustling around her face. "We haven't done anything conventionally from the start."

"You've got me there, lady." He'd read her eyes so well in bringing down Chavez and Rick thought he could read her now, still he wanted to hear the words. "You still haven't answered."

Then it hit him. He still hadn't given her much of a real proposal, either. Just the under-pressure "I love you" they'd shared in passing.

He stopped the swing. Stared into her eyes. He needed to make this count. "All of these plans, they feel right, being a part of a group, something big again. But without you, I wouldn't have been able to wrap my brain around the possibility. God, Nola, you've given me so much. I just hope I can give you as much in return, because without you none of it means anything."

He cupped her face. "Nola, I love you. I wish there were fancier words, but I'm a plainspoken man. I'm also a man you can count on. I don't quit. My love for you is forever."

"Wow."

He laughed. "I've made you speechless. That's quite a feat."

She pressed her hands to his chest and kissed him on the mouth, "I love you," on the cheeks, "I love you," on the eyes and the forehead, "I love you!"

"And thank goodness you weren't speechless for long."

"I guess this means we are officially and fully engaged?"

"Absolutely. We had milk shakes for Thanksgiving." He took her hand in his, linking their fingers and holding on tight. For a lifetime. "I was thinking perhaps we could shop for a diamond for Christmas."

"Sounds like a plan to me, my love. Definitely sounds like a plan."

* * * * *

Don't miss Catherine Mann's next release,
available March 2007 from Silhouette Desire.

New York Times *bestselling author*
Linda Lael Miller is back with a
new romance featuring the heartwarming
McKettrick family
from Silhouette Special Edition.

SIERRA'S HOMECOMING
by Linda Lael Miller

On sale December 2006,
wherever books are sold.

Turn the page for a sneak preview!

Soft, smoky music poured into the room.

The next thing she knew, Sierra was in Travis's arms, close against that chest she'd admired earlier, and they were slow dancing.

Why didn't she pull away?

"Relax," he said. His breath was warm in her hair.

She giggled, more nervous than amused. What was the matter with her? She was attracted to Travis, had been from the first, and he was clearly attracted to her. They were both adults. Why not enjoy a little slow dancing in a ranch-house kitchen?

Because slow dancing led to other things. She took a step back and felt the counter flush against her lower back. Travis naturally came with her, since they were holding hands and he had one arm around her waist.

Simple physics.

Then he kissed her.

Physics again—this time, not so simple.

"Yikes," she said, when their mouths parted.

He grinned. "Nobody's ever said that after I kissed them."

She felt the heat and substance of his body pressed against hers. "It's going to happen, isn't it?" she heard herself whisper.

"Yep," Travis answered.

"But not tonight," Sierra said on a sigh.

"Probably not," Travis agreed.

"When, then?"

He chuckled, gave her a slow, nibbling kiss. "Tomorrow morning," he said. "After you drop Liam off at school."

"Isn't that…a little…soon?"

"Not soon enough," Travis answered, his voice husky. "Not nearly soon enough."

SPECIAL EDITION™

Silhouette Special Edition brings you a
heartwarming new story from the *New York Times*
bestselling author of *McKettrick's Choice*

LINDA LAEL MILLER

Sierra's Homecoming

Sierra's Homecoming
follows the parallel lives
of two McKettrick women,
living their lives in the
same house but
generations apart,
each with a special son
and an unlikely new
romance.

December 2006

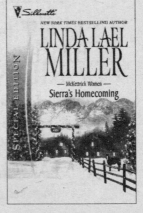

HARLEQUIN® *Romance*®

**From the Heart.
For the Heart.**

Get swept away into the Outback
with two of Harlequin Romance's
top authors.

Coming in December...

Claiming the
Cattleman's Heart
BY BARBARA HANNAY

And in January don't miss...

Outback Man Seeks Wife
BY MARGARET WAY

REQUEST YOUR FREE BOOKS!

2 FREE NOVELS
PLUS 2 FREE GIFTS!

Silhouette® Romantic

SUSPENSE

Sparked by Danger, Fueled by Passion!

COMING NEXT MONTH